Hooked by the Stars

Pueo's Voyage to Hawai'i

by

Aline LaForge

Wise Bird Books LLC

Hooked by the Stars

Pueo's Voyage to Hawai'i

Hooked by the Stars: Pueo's Voyage to Hawaiʻi
First edition Printed in the United States of America

LaForge, Aline
Hooked by the Stars
ISBN: 978-0-9907827-9-7
LCCN:2017909747

BISAC
4.0.1.6.5.0.0 Hawaii
FIC009030 Fiction/Fantasy/Historical
FIC051000 Fiction/Cultural Heritage
YAF014000 Young Adult Fiction/Diversity and Multicultural

Cover and Interior Block Print Illustrations by Dietrich Varez
courtesy of Karen Kaufman, The Magic Mo, ArtPrintsHawaii.com
Interior and Cover design and photo by Aline LaForge
Cover Background photograph Palomar 12 Star,
by Hubble Telescope courtesy of NASA images, ESA/NASA.
Pueo Project Logo courtesy of Dr. J. Cotín, Pueo Hui, UH at Manoa.

Pueo's Voyage Map by Aline LaForge.
Base map source by Tentotwo [Creative Commons BY-SA 3.0]
Canoe by Hannah McLain.
Polynesian navigation device from
S. Percy Smith - www.nzetc.org Public Domain.

Published by Wise Bird Books LLC
PO Box 433
Fruita, CO, 81521

Pueo's Voyage to Hawai'i

"Aloha" means to hear what is not said,
to see what cannot be seen and to know the unknowable.
From H.R.S.§5-7.5, the Aloha Spirit Law.

Meli's Question

People are always coming and going at Aunty Min's *hale*, filling the driveway with their old jalopies. They bring baskets of food, play their *'ukuleles* and guitars, and sing. If *keiki* come with their parents, we run around and have plenty of fun, good small-kid time. When only grown-ups are at the *hale*, the women chatter like chickens, and some of the men laugh too loud. I might as well be invisible as I weave through the forest of their legs and elbows. They don't notice me, even when they step on my toes.

Today I'm underfoot and ignored, so I slink away across the pasture to a secret hideaway, a nook high in the old stone wall. An owl glides across the open field below me, searching for dinner. I wonder if there's a nest at the bottom of the hill. Standing in my rock chair, arms outstretched, I pretend to fly with him.

I don't notice the boy walking through the tall grass until he is halfway across the clearing.

"*Ho'ōho*, halloo," he calls out.

"*Hūi*," I wave, then tuck my hands under my arms, embarrassed that this boy saw me dancing with the owl.

"Can I sit with you?" He peers up at me through black framed glasses. The round lenses are so big they reflect the sky, and I can't see his eyes.

"I guess so." I move over to give him my seat and study the top of his head as he climbs up the wall. His hair is not like mine. It's short and curly. And his skin is much darker, like the heartwood of the *koa* tree. I wonder which island his family comes from.

"Ah, dis rock's a good perch. Sound like a party up at da *hale*." He points up the hill with his glasses, then begins to wipe the lenses with his shirttail.

"Just grown-ups today," I say.

"Dat's no fun." He has the most intense dark brown eyes I've ever seen. When he crossed the field I figured he was a kid, but now his eyes say otherwise and I blush. He must be about eighteen, maybe younger.

"Why you sittin' alone?"

"I'm so short, nobody..." I start to say, but he's no taller than I am. The lump in my throat forces me into an awkward silence.

"Yeah, know what you mean." His words come slow and careful. "No one notices you. Kinda lonely when you in da way, right?"

"Yes!" He's not upset, so I start all over again. "I'm Meli, what's your name?"

"Li'ulā." He slaps his thigh and chuckles. "But you should call me Loloa."

"There's a kid at school who calls me that. Mean, don't you think? She doesn't have to remind me that I'm the shortest girl in class."

"Some of us never gonna be tall, right?"

"That's what my Aunty Min says."

"Well, your Aunty must be a smart lady. Loloa's just a nickname, okay? Callin' you tall when you short, no big deal. Don't let da teasin' bother you, Meli."

"Do you live upcountry, Loloa?" Only a couple paths come around the bottom of this pasture, and I've never seen him in town before.

"Nope, just passin' through. I like to move around" he says, wiggling around on the stone. "So I give you some advice, Meli. When you're with tall people, do what I do."

"What's that?"

"Find somewhere high to sit." He laughs like he has just told me the funniest joke. I giggle nervously, pretending to understand. "No, I'm serious, Meli. Dat way, you look 'em in da eye, and dey forget how short you are."

"Oh." I want Loloa to stay, but I don't know what we can talk about. Maybe if I ask about his family. In Hawai'i that's sure to keep him here awhile as he recites the names of his father's fathers, and his mother's mothers, back through the generations. Before I can get a word out, he jumps from the wall in a single leap, and adjusts his glasses on his nose. Tongue-tied I blurt, "Can we be friends?" followed by a silent groan. Just when I want to look more grown-up, I sound like a dumb kid.

He laughs in a nice way, so maybe asking for his friendship was not a *keiki* question. "You bet." With a wave he strides away. "I'll be seein' you, Meli. *Aloha.*"

"*Aloha*, Loloa." I wave from the top of the wall. Once he disappears in the tall grass I scramble down and run back to the *hale*. He's right! The rail on the *lānai* is just about the right height for me to join the party.

*   *   *

When my mom disappeared, an unwelcome creature moved into my broken heart. A shadowy thing that slithered about and smothered me with loneliness. I try to cling to the memories I have of happier times with her, waiting for the first evening star and dancing in the kitchen. The brightness of those thoughts helps keep that ghost away, but other times I am like a bare light bulb. When I stop to wonder why she left me, the switch is flipped and my brain turns off. I guess that's why Aunty Min hardly ever talks about the night I was dropped on her doorstep, and the darkness of the days that followed.

Mom's not dead, at least I don't think she is, so for a while I am *keiki hānai*, an adopted kid. I live near Honoka'a on the island of Hawai'i with my Aunty Min, who is very old, and her two sisters, who are not quite so old. Our *hale*, what you call a house, is perched on the edge of a gulch overlooking a wild valley. Far below, a mountain stream tumbles out to the ocean.

Aunty Min likes to "talk story." In Hawai'i that means she shares an everyday event, like going to the store, but instead of plopping a sack of food down in the kitchen with a simple "I done the shopping," she will weave the changes in the weather, the family and friends she meets on the way there and back, and the fruit and meats she buys into a colorful tale. You can hear this gift of storytelling in all of her tales, except when I ask about my mama. Then Aunty Min's words fly by like a bird. She always starts and ends the same way with nothing new in between, so I know the words by heart.

"Long time ago, when sugarcane first came to our island, the fields were worked by Hawai'ians, men like your *kupuna kāne* and his father before him. As time went by, the owners wanted more land and more cane, so they brought in workers from all over the world. What sugar gave our people was not always sweet. Those companies changed the towns and the land. Most people, no matter how hard they worked, didn't make enough, while a few idle ones had too much. Misery can turn a person's life upside-down." She snaps her fingers and says "just like that," before she continues. "In 1929 times were hard. Late one night I heard an old truck roll down the driveway, followed by a knock on my door. There you stood in the glare of the headlights, just a bitty thing. As your mama handed you over, a man's voice come out of the darkness. 'Hey, gotta go. Don't miss your ride.' The truck backed away, and she shouted out the window, 'Meli honey, I'll see you again.' That man helped your mama slip onto a boat. She sailed away, and nobody heard from her since."

At the ending, the sorrow in her voice is deep and never changes. Her eyes lose their sparkle, so I don't dare ask for more. Why that night ever came to pass is a mystery.

I was seven when I came to live with the aunties. It's not unusual for a kid to be handed off to an aunty or *kupuna*. Someone will always make room for a *keiki*, a little kid. Even though six years have passed, I don't think I've grown more than a couple inches. As far as I can tell since I arrived, Aunty Min hasn't changed much either. Her flowered dresses are loose and always pretty pastel colors. She says a lady shouldn't dress too loud. She wears her long black hair coiled in a bun on the back of her head. My hair grows fast, long enough that she braids it for me on school days, but my bones don't seem to grow. I'm still as short as the day I arrived.

"That's okay, Meli," Aunty Min said. "Some of our people aren't real tall, but we have big hearts."

For a long time I was so lonely it hurt. My ears would ring and everything looked dim and fuzzy, like I was living underwater. When I was at home, I could sneak away to my room and wait until the feeling passed, but school was different. The only place to hide in class was with my head on my desk, hoping nobody noticed. That worked until the kids in class started to tease me. I would wake to the sound of Teacher slapping her palm with her ruler and cringe because I knew what was next.

Last year Teacher rapped my knuckles with her ruler almost every day. Finally, on a Friday morning, she gave me an envelope with Aunty's name printed in bold letters and sent me home. I found Aunty Min on the back *lānai*, beating rugs over the porch rail.

"What's this? You home early, Meli?" she said.

I hung my head like a scolded puppy as she tore open the envelope. By the look on Aunty's face, I knew Teacher's note was bad news.

"Well," she said as she shoved the letter deep into her apron pocket, "let's just say that teacher don't know the whole story. You gonna grow up to be a fine girl, Honey Bee." She wrapped me in a hug, then straightened me up by the shoulders. "Be proud of who you are, Meli, and always stand tall. I'm gonna teach you how to sing for our *'aumakua*, our family guardian, so this don't happen again."

The bench outside the kitchen door creaked as Aunty eased herself down and patted the peeling painted slats beside her, a signal that I was about to get a little home-learning.

"Every family has an *'aumakua*, a guardian. Our protector is Pueo, a name Hawai'ian people gave to the owls. Just like in the old days, Meli, you must honor your ancestors and follow their ways. The old ones will help whenever that lonely darkness starts creepin' around."

My feet tingled when she told me about all of the people who had walked this land before me. Family is important. I listened close as Aunty told me more.

"Long time ago, long before any people from Europe came to this island, Pueo chose a woman in our family. He decided to be her protector and guide, a special gift, not to be taken lightly. Always show respect, don't ever ask Pueo's help for silly things. But when the shadow comes and your heart fills with worry, Pueo will bring you courage."

Then Aunty taught me a *mele*, a song to call the owl. I memorized the words that had been passed down through countless generations. She said my *'aumakua* would always hear me, even if I sang to myself. After that day on the bench with Aunty Min, Teacher never had to send another note.

If the darkness tries to creep up at school, I clamp my hands over my ears and listen hard for Aunty Min's lilting voice. In the classroom, I whisper the *mele*, at home, I sing along. The ancient meaning of the words brings my *'aumakua* to me. Pueo dives in with his fierce eyes and sharp talons. With Pueo's help I chase away the sadness. Instead of a scary shadow, a glow shines in my heart, small and pure like the flame of a burning *kukui* nut.

My favorite place is anywhere Aunty Min sits to tell a story from the old days, a time when everyone was touched by magic and not every mystery was solved. I can listen to those ancient tales over and over again. Today, a rare day when only the two of us are home, I find Aunty out on the *lānai*. I drop my book bag and settle on the porch mat next to her chair. With ankles crossed on the footstool her bare feet wag back and forth in the cool afternoon breeze.

"Aunty, can I ask you something?"

"Hmm?" She sets aside her tea cup.

"Every time you tell our *'aumakua* story I hear something new. How can that be?"

"Stories explain the world around us, Meli. As you grow up, the stories grow up too. Always changing just like you."

Now that I am almost fourteen, my book bag is much heavier than when I was a *keiki*. Teacher says if I learn everything in those books I will understand that the world is much bigger than our island. Today I have a question about the owls we call Pueo. Maybe Aunty Min will know the answer.

"In science class Teacher told us what the people who study birds say about Pueo. Did you know that owls on other continents only hunt at night, but our Pueo flies and hunts during the day? And they eat rats and even other birds. And the owls on Hawai'i are..." I try to connect my brain to my tongue. I already forgot the word, but I bet it will be on the next test.

"They are, well, special. Over a hundred years ago a biologist sailed here on a ship. He discovered that Hawai'ian Pueo are different from all the other short-eared owls. Pueo only lives here, on our islands. They've been here more than a thousand years and you won't find an owl exactly like them anywhere else in the whole wide world." Pausing just long enough to gasp for air, I go on, "But how can that be? Our islands are in the middle of the Pacific Ocean. I even asked Teacher, 'How did two owls find our island and settle to raise baby owls?' She didn't know. Do you?"

"Pueo?" Aunty Min chuckles and tilts her head to watch a rainbow dance between the clouds and ocean before she continues, "There is one story of how Pueo came to Hawai'i that belongs to your family." She settles into the cushions of her chair, straightens her faded flower dress, and takes a sip of tea.

"Years ago your Uncle Kō and I sailed to our home islands far to the south. We stayed with a *kupuna*, an elder in our family. A long tale takes time, so every few nights she would tell us of the journey of Pueo, the same way I will tell his story to you. Pueo's adventure began in a small village on Nuku Hiva, the largest of the northern isles of Hiva, what your teacher would call the Marquesas Islands. Life back then was different from today. Everyone believed in magic and the power of dreams. In that village there lived a man and a woman, Kaʻimi and Kāulamana, sorcerers who walked with the spirits of the ancestors, the gods and goddesses. Their sacred work and the words they brought back from their journeys were respected, sometimes even feared. Their wisdom guided the *aliʻi*, the village chiefs, who were very powerful. Back in those days the people obeyed the *aliʻi* without question. Life in the village was not easy, but the men and women worked and played, and loved their *ʻohana*." Aunty Min squints. I know her gaze is searching for that time long ago in a far-away place. This is my cue that the story is about to begin. I pull together a pile of pillows and snuggle in.

"Let's see if I remember how Pueo found Hawaiʻi." Setting her cup aside, she smooths the wrinkles on the back of one hand with the finger-tips of the other as she gathers her thoughts. "Ah yes, the tale begins with Lani at her favorite pool below the waterfall..."

Aunty's Story

Lani tasted sweetness in the water as she swam through the mist near the waterfall. Rain clouds gathered every day high on the mountain. The forest, thick with sandalwood trees and spikes of ginger flowers, combed droplets from the rain clouds. The sparkling water streamed through a narrow valley until spreading at a broad stone ledge. The droplets jumped into the air one last time before pounding the boulders below with a roar.

The rock ledge pushed back the dark forest. Below the green canopy Lani floated on her back. Eyes closed, she drifted with the current from the deep end of the pool towards the low rock dam. Birds played in the dappled sunlight high in the trees. Their melodic calls joined the rhythmic beat of the waterfall. Earlier the song of the stream had been drowned out by a crowd of boys and girls splashing and screaming, but everyone else had left, returning to work in the village or the fields. Only Lani had stayed behind.

The voice of the stream changed as the water gurgled through the dam. Lani dropped one leg to let her foot sink to the bottom. Her toe slid across a smooth stone in the shallows. She stood and wiped the water from her forehead with the back of her arm. As her eyes adjusted from the bright sunlight to the shadows of the deep green forest, the grass parted in front of her, and a round face with dark eyes stared back.

Startled, she scuttled backwards away from the stream bank. Her father's warning rang in her ears, "Don't be caught alone at the pool!" Ka'imi had shouted as she ran off with her friends that morning. Her father had told her about a strange canoe landing on the far side of their island. "Warriors from another island are stalking through the jungle."

She stumbled and fell in the shallow water, trembling as the figure rose from the shadows and cackled.

"Hoo hoo Lani, got you." Leaping out of the bushes, the young man startled the birds. They scattered, their wings like clapping hands against the jungle undergrowth.

"*Ho'okolohe,* Kekoa, you are such a rascal." She stood, shaking her fist at him in mock anger. "Your silly game is not funny."

"Is too." Kekoa hooted as he ran toward the path, looking back to be sure Lani took the bait.

She splashed across the stream, scrambled over the slippery rocks on the bank, and raced down the trail after Kekoa. When she caught him, first she would pinch him hard for scaring her, and then they would both fall down laughing.

Kekoa was a little older than Lani, but no one watching him lope through the jungle would guess his age by the pranks he played on her. Playmates since childhood and still close, they were no longer *keiki*, carefree young children. Kekoa had moved into the men's *hale* a couple years ago. He was strong enough to haul rocks for a house platform and dig to make clearings for *'ulu,* the breadfruit trees.

Lani lived in the women's *hale*, with the aunties and all the *keiki*. She learned how to prepare food, weave mats and baskets, and watch after the youngest *keiki*. Whenever she could sneak away from her chores, Lani went fishing with her father Ka'imi or hiked alone in the hills above the village.

Lani had always liked Kekoa because he was different. Short and stout like an old tree, he was usually serious except when he caught Lani alone. Then he played games and smirked his silly smile.

Girls her age were starting to pay attention to the young men. The aunties said that a young woman should judge the character of a man by watching how he takes care of himself and how he treats others. Kekoa was bold when he pestered Lani, but timid with the open ocean. She didn't know why he was so careful. He would spear fish or cast nets in the bays protected by reefs, yet he never ventured beyond even in a canoe. Every *keiki* knew not to turn their back on the waves, but anyone who didn't swim out to the diving rocks, go fishing out beyond the reef, or paddle outriggers across the open waters between the islands was bound to be teased. Although wary of the ocean, Kekoa wasn't afraid of the village bullies. When a person with a mean heart started picking on a *keiki*, Kekoa would step in to protect them. If the bully was smart, he'd duck out of the way. Some boys tormented others with their crude tricks. What girl would be impressed by that? Those boys tried too hard to be noticed.

Kekoa didn't run wild with the other young men, wrestling and tussling like a pack of dogs. Lani admired the way Kekoa took time to sit with the *kūpuna*. He listened when the old ones shared family stories or tales about the spirits and ancestors. These elders had gained wisdom from their life experiences. Their words fed his imagination and guided his behavior. He was wiser for the time he spent with them.

As Lani dashed after him down the valley trail, the distance between them grew. By the next stream crossing she had lost sight of Kekoa. A sharp pain jabbed under her ribs and slowed her to a jog. She stopped, panting, with both hands on her knees. Lani waited for the side-ache to fade away. She took a deep breath and sighed. An unfamiliar ache still gripped her somewhere between her stomach and her heart.

Lani startled at the sound of someone clearing her throat. She looked up, dismayed to find Miki rooted in the middle of the path. Hands on her hips, Miki stood a full head taller and twice as wide as Lani.

"I couldn't believe my eyes. Even with his stubby legs you didn't catch him."

"Catch who, Miki?" Lani didn't like the idea of Miki spying on their private games.

"Kekoa, of course. He was watching after you gave up. What a little trickster he is."

"He was long gone before I stopped." Lani waited for Miki to be polite and step aside so she could continue down the trail. Instead Miki stepped forward to increase her taunting, inches from Lani's face.

"No he wasn't. He was in the bushes over there."

Lani's glance followed Miki's pointing finger. Had Kekoa been watching her again?

"Don't worry, he's gone now. You almost caught him. Why were you chasing him anyway?" Miki planted her feet wider while she waited for an answer that did not come.

"Well, at least you run faster than you paddle," Miki continued. "You and your crew of misfits made a mess of the village trading trip the other day."

Lani opened her mouth, wanting to protest Miki's insult, but stopped herself. Miki was always looking for an argument.

"I guess that's true." Lani crossed her arms and looked away. She hoped Miki would take a hint and leave. Miki's hips and elbows blocked the trail. Lani didn't want a fight.

Miki arched her eyebrows. If she could goad Lani into making excuses for her friends, then she could have some real fun. But Lani pressed her lips tight.

A gentle breath of cool air flowed down the valley trail. No hot words flowed. Not today.

Miki snorted, "I've got more important things to do than argue with a *keiki*." She pushed past Lani. "Out of my way."

Lani wondered if Miki had actually seen Kekoa. Didn't matter anyway. Miki would pull aside the next villager on the trail to gossip. 'Did you see long-leg Lani chasing after that little man Kekoa?'

"When will Kekoa grow up?" Lani asked the spirits in the forest canopy before she walked on. "Teasing is for *keiki*." She blushed at the thought of how easily Kekoa lured her into his games.

On the path back to the village she stopped at the ruins of an old abandoned *hale*. The spirit of a *kupuna*, a grandmother, spoke aloud to her from the rubble. Her words reminded Lani about judging people's qualities.

"Hōkūlani," this *kupuna* had always used her full name, "be mindful of how you value a person. The strong become weak, the tall bend over, even beauty fades, but kindness remains and grows. And although you might not recognize the gift, every kind deed is greeted by a reward."

Kekoa's teasing wasn't exactly a kind deed, but maybe in his own awkward way he was attracted to her. Lani wriggled her toes in the cool mud, closed her eyes, and took in the heady fragrance from the spikes of ginger in bloom on both sides of the path. Warmth spread across her face and chest as her daydream progressed.

She opened her eyes and asked the forest spirits, "Could I be his reward?" She immediately regretted the question. She knew the spirits had more important matters than her desires.

To long for the embrace of Kekoa's arms was a childish daydream compared to the magic of visions. When she was older, perhaps the spirits would speak to her in the same way they did to her father Ka'imi. Even though she left offerings at the *heiau*, the stone alters, and chanted the *mele*, the songs her father taught her, Lani never heard the spirit voices or saw their faces. They were probably waiting for her to grow up. She would have to remember not to ask them silly questions.

Lani's dreams were still tied to the earth, her common needs and everyday worries. She knew her father's visions were different. He could see vivid scenes illuminated by the gods, goddesses, and spirits. Ka'imi walked through the mists separating this living world from the villages of the ancestors and the realm of the gods.

Lazing in the cool shadows didn't last for long. Oh no! How could she have forgotten? All the other girls had left the pool and returned to the village hours ago to help the aunties prepare bark for *tapas*. She ran down the trail at an easy lope instead of the frantic pace of the earlier chase. Kekoa had better look out because one of these days she would catch him.

Lani rushed around a huge boulder on the mountain side of the village and scattered a group of young pigs from their mother. Amid the squealing *pua'a* she called out, "I'm here to help you."

A group of girls sat in the shade with the *mākuahines* and *kūpunas*, the women of the village. They chattered as they worked on a pile of plants they had gathered for barkcloth. With strong, skilled fingers the older women peeled the white inner bark from shoots of *wauke*, the paper mulberry. Freshly cut branches were slit lengthwise, then held between their feet while they used both thumbs to skillfully peel the bark off in one long piece. Younger girls, too small to do this chore, were busy shredding strips from young *'ulu*, the breadfruit, into strands of fibers. Their circle was closed. Lani stood awkwardly on the outside.

"Plenty of hands here already," the oldest *kupuna*, one who had chided Lani just last week for laziness, waved her hand to send Lani away.

Embarrassed to be idle while others were hard at work, a frown wrinkled Lani's brow. *Kupuna's* rejection was worse than a scolding. She apologized and asked if she could help, but the women continued to ignore her. At moments like this Lani wished she had a mother, not just *kūpuna* in this circle. A mother might overlook her flaws. Nothing for her to do but leave. Lani shuffled as she considered which trail to take away from the village. Back into the valley or up into the hills? No one saw the wide grin spread across her face as she remembered a secret from a few days ago. She had discovered a bird nest hidden in the grass high on the mountain and counted seven perfect eggs. By now baby birds might be waiting. She flew up the ridge trail hoping to find new fuzzy friends.

Ka'imi's Dream

While Lani ran through the mountain clearing in search of the hidden nest, Ka'imi sat in the shade where the cool forest gave way to the bright white sand. The shadows of the clouds played across the dark water between the reef and a distant island. In one hand he held a rough rock. With the other he worked the tip of a shell fishhook back and forth across the stone, its sharp point almost finished. His toes dug in the warm sand. Gazing at the hook, mesmerized by the colors of the shell, he drifted off into a dream world where he stood alone on a beach a moment before sunrise. The sea and the sky kissed like giant pearls. Pale blue, pink, and white touched briefly with the horizon vanishing between them. While his mind wandered, his fingers continued working the shell.

Setting aside the finished fishhook, he began another. As the next hook took shape, his thoughts strayed to the night and a recent vision. Lost in his dream world, Ka'imi didn't notice Lani sit down across from him. The gentle tapping of someone striking a shell brought him back.

"Ah, Lani, I didn't hear you join me. What brings you to the beach?"

"I spotted you from the ridge trail."

"I'm making these for Ikaika." He held up the half-finished fishhook. "My able young friend leaves tomorrow on a fishing trip. He makes beautiful bone hooks, but he has less patience for small tools and delicate shells."

"I hope Ikaika will like this," Lani said. She deftly flipped the shell and began to work the other side, the rough shape of a hook emerging. "It's good that his heart is as big as the rest of him," she added. Ikaika was not only strong, he was massive, and dwarfed her father when they were together in a fishing canoe.

"Why were you up on the ridge trail?" Ka'imi asked.

"I found a nest, built on the ground, not in a tree. I hoped that the eggs had hatched, then I could see what kind of bird puts their nest in the grass. I'll have to go back again in a few days. Is this a new mat?" She fingered the edge of the *moena*. The woven leaves were still pliable and fragrant.

"Yes, I traded a basket of *uhu* for a *moena*. A good deal for me," Ka'imi grinned. "Lani, are you interested in a story? I have a vision to share."

"Of course." Her father's stories from dream time were exciting. Lani sat back on her feet and continued shaping the fishhook for Ikaika.

"You are the first to hear these words. Last week, one after another, these visions came to me. When I crossed over into dream time, I returned to the same place and continued on the journey that was revealed the night before. The first night was nothing unusual. Ikaika and I dropped our hooks out beyond the reef. Our long lines trailed behind the canoe. Then, all of a sudden, we were in the dark-blue ocean far to the north where we never go."

"You and Ikaika often fish together. Maybe that part of your dream means you will go on a longer trip with Ikaika, to look for bigger fish?"

"A longer trip, yes, but with more than just Ikaika. The next night I sailed with a handful of men in a large canoe. I was the only one casting, a single line with one hook. After a while the line grew taut and I strained against the pull. You know how some dreams are bigger than life, everything out of proportion, nothing is the right size?"

As the story unfolded, Ka'imi's hands began to fly in the air between them. "The hook seemed too small and the fishing line was as thick as my fist." Lani pulled back as her father shook his arm in front of her face. "To gain control I grasped the line with both hands, for it seemed as if a great beast tugged from the other end. I awoke in a cold sweat, my fingers wound around an imaginary fishing line."

"Why would a giant from the deep swallow such a tiny lure?" Lani asked as she turned over the the hook in her hand, trying to imagine Ka'imi's beast.

"Because the giant," Ka'imi paused, "wanted to be caught." Lani pondered the idea while tapping away at the shell. Enormous creatures lurked in the ocean, but she didn't like to hear about them. She often swam out to the diving rock, so she didn't spend much time imagining the monsters in the depths of the dark blue waters.

"The following night my fishing line curved away from the *pola.*" Ka'imi wondered if Lani had seen the type of canoe he was talking about. "You know, the deck on a double-hulled canoe."

Lani nodded. "My friends and I went to the long beach to see the voyaging canoe. We kept the craftsmen busy with all of our questions, and after awhile they chased us off so they could get back to work. They are almost finished."

"Good for you," he laughed. "Not for being a pest, but I'm pleased you are curious about the canoe. So, there I was on the *pola.* I held on as the voyaging canoe sped along. The winds howled and both sails were taut. A yank on my fishing line almost pulled my arms off, but I held tight. Hand-over-hand, I hauled my catch up from the depths. Instead of the nose of a giant fish hooked on the end of my line, one that could feed a whole village, the tip of an enormous mountain poked out of the sea before me. I had fished up an island!"

"An island? Like in the legends? I have heard a story about catching an island before, from the oldest of the *kūpuna.*" Carried along by Ka'imi's joy, Lani asked, "What did the next dream show you?"

"That night the island rose from the ocean. The land's roots started deep, and grew high above the water with fire and steam. Two mountain tops gleamed brilliant white. Crimson rivers flowed from the ridges to the sea. Forests of tall trees covered the black soil on the lower slopes. Even now, sharing these words with you, I am so excited. If you had watched me sleeping that night, I'm sure I twitched like a dog chasing a pig in his dreams."

"In the last vision we sailed close to the island. The canoe rode high on the swells before a great wind. Dark cliffs loomed along the shore. Where would we land? Swept along by the force of the winds, the canoe sped along the coast. Waves crashed over shallow reefs, breaking off chunks of coral, grinding and tossing them toward the shore. Past a gap in the reef I saw the crescent of a white coral beach. We pulled the sails and the canoe glided into a narrow bay where the waters were calm."

Ka'imi's story ended abruptly and Lani searched his face. His eyebrows knit together. Ka'imi was lost in worried thoughts. Out of respect for his musings she remained silent. She knew that Ka'imi's dream was the last in a series of events that were set in motion years ago. The *ali'i* had been waiting for this vision.

The troubled times had started on a southern archipelago when a powerful *ali'i*, a village chief, was killed. Warring factions from his family suspected a village on their island harbored the murderers, but their mayhem soon spread north, to the neighboring islands. Lesser chiefs reacted and sent warriors to raid other villages. Victims were taken for revenge and rumors of human sacrifice planted the seeds of terror. Warfare threatened certain lineages with extinction. The *ali'i* of Lani's village met in secret to decide which family lines would be protected and how they would find their new island. They drank their *'awa* and waited for the goddess to guide them.

In public they declared that the village would build a voyaging canoe. They chose a *kahuna* who was experienced in consulting the spirits of the forest and guiding the work of building canoes. Two enormous trees were carefully selected, blessed, and after conducting a ceremony of gratitude, chopped down. The *ali'i* directed the craftsmen to begin shaping the *wā'a*, the canoe. The task to hollow out the logs took over twelve moon cycles. While the hulls took shape, more trees were blessed. Cross beams were needed to join the hulls together and two masts were stepped, one in front of the other, in the center of the *pola*, the deck. The finished *pola* was as wide as three tall men lying head to toe, and the hulls extended four times as long. The workers were almost finished with the last task, shaping the *mo'o*, side boards that kept high waves from washing into the hulls. The voyaging canoe was too heavy to be paddled. She would be powered by the wind. While the men worked on the *wā'a*, a group of women prepared *lau hala*. Unlike wall or floor mats, the sail mats had a tight weave, and the leaves of the *hala* tree were strong enough to catch and hold the wind even when soaking wet. The work was almost done. The last preparations for the naming ceremony were complete. The *kahuna* had chosen to call the double-hulled voyaging canoe Ho'ololi, because the journey would transform both the crew that sailed and the loved ones they left behind.

"My vision of the new island is complete." Lani was jarred by Ka'imi's proclamation.

"Did you dream last night?" Lani asked, rubbing the barbed point of the hook between her finger and thumb.

"No. I still need to find the path of stars that will guide us to our new home." The *ali'i* kept many secrets, and Ka'imi immediately regretted his words. His vision secured his place on the voyaging canoe. Surely the *ali'i* would select Lani to join him. She was the only child of her mother's lineage, an ancient and powerful family. Although the voyage to the new island would be dangerous, Lani faced greater risks if she stayed behind. How would he protect her?

"Don't worry father," Lani rose from the mat and dusted the silvery shell powder from the dark skin of her thigh.

"But the star song is still missing."

"With the favor of the gods you'll find the stars soon." She offered a perfect fishhook to Ka'imi and started to walk away, then remembered to leave him with a kind word. "Thank you for letting me be the first to hear about the island."

"Thank you," Ka'imi lifted the hook to his brow, palms pressed together, before placing it with the others.

Setting aside his tools, Ka'imi leaned back on the mat. Palm fronds rustled above in the breeze. Their sensuous dance made his eyelids heavy. He rolled to his side. The pungent leaves of the new mat caressed his cheek. As he closed his eyes, a bird warbled, almost like a woman singing to him. The tones mingled with the sound of the surf and the wind. Was someone nearby? He propped himself up on an elbow and looked around. Nobody was on the beach. He shut his eyes again, not to sleep, but to listen. Ka'imi was sure the source of the song was no ordinary woman, and she only sang when his eyes were closed. Could this be Hina, the goddess?

Words sprang from the melody. Hina chanted the names of stars he had never seen before. A new sky spread before him as Hina shared her wisdom, the wayfinding stars that were missing from his dream. Ka'imi began to sing along with the goddess, repeating the star names, their compass direction, and the times they rose and set. The gift of the star song affirmed that the voyage sailed with the favor of the gods. He would share his vision of the new island with the *kūpuna* and give Hina's chant to Kele, the navigator and teacher. Kele knew how to read the sky and follow the ocean's paths. He would use Hina's star song to guide them to the island hooked by Ka'imi's dreams.

Once the words were memorized, Ka'imi sat up and continued the chant in a booming voice. He didn't notice an old woman as she picked her way through the rocks, shuffling under the weight of a carrying basket bulging with fruit. Setting her burden down above the wet sand the *kupuna* rested both hands on her lower back and stretched with a groan.

"Who is singing? Ah, is that Ka'imi up there in the shade?" As she listened the cadence of the chant reminded her of bold canoe trips from her youth. But her voyaging days were long behind her. Too old for sailing, a pang of nostalgia for more adventurous times washed over her. She spoke aloud to nobody in particular, a little resentment tinging her voice.

"So this old one lugs fruit out of the forest, dries and packs the gourds, only to feed these young voyagers." Then she clucked to herself, thankful Ka'imi was too far away to hear. It was not a kind heart that had wagged her tongue.

"Let the selection be guided by the heavens" the *kupuna* apologized to any of the ancestors who might be listening.

She stooped and lifted her basket, adjusting the strap to fit comfortably against her old bones before she headed up the beach toward the village. After a lifetime on the island she knew most everyone's secrets, even Ka'imi's. Life had given him blessings and then taken them away. He once had a family. Lani was Ka'imi's only child. His wife, that enchanted woman, had left them both for reasons this *kupuna* would never speak of. Soon after that stormy night, Lani and Ka'imi had disappeared. After time had passed with no sign of Ka'imi and his daughter, or word of them from travelers, the villagers worried for their wellbeing. One day they paddled back into the bay as if nothing had happened. Everyone knew Ka'imi had brought Lani back because she was growing up and should be raised by the women. Even though she had a flighty way about her, the *kupuna* had to admit that Lani had grown into a beautiful girl. To some it might have looked as if all was well with Ka'imi, but this *kupuna* knew better. He still yearned for his wife, his lost love. Ka'imi kept to himself. Other than fishing with Ikaika, he spent most of his time with the ancestors. Yes, if Ka'imi was singing a star song the voyaging canoe would soon sail. People who left on these trips rarely came back. Their fate fell to the hands of the gods and their future remained a mystery to those left behind. To help the voyagers was an honor, no matter how small her contribution. Later that evening she would take Ka'imi some of this fresh fruit and share a kind word with him. As the *kupuna* ambled off into the forest, the change in her heart had lightened the weight of her burden.

Ho'ololi Change

Flowers drifted around Lani in the pool at the base of the waterfall. Their spicy scents clung to her skin. If only the roar of the pounding water could wash away the pain of Kekoa's questions.

This morning had started out like any other day. She found Kekoa down at the cove. They swam inside the reef and chased colorful fish around the coral. Lani drifted further out where she could see a group of friends diving from the rock that jutted from the water, far out beyond the reef. When she glanced back, Kekoa was swimming toward the beach. Lani followed after Kekoa. With the chase through the forest still fresh in her mind she wanted to spend the day alone with him, to make her feelings clear to him and plant the seed for them to grow together. While she focused on Kekoa, Lani forgot all about how Ka'imi's vision might change her plans.

Once the sand shimmered in the sun they moved into the cool shade of the forest, looking for ripe guava fruit along the trail. By midday, the steamy heat pushed them up-valley to the long pool below the waterfall. Sitting in the shallows across from each other, they wove flowers and leaves into garlands, laughing and joking, playing word games with riddles and songs.

"Hokulani, you mean so much to me." Kekoa's dark eyes held Lani's gaze. "I can't imagine a day going by without you. Please tell me the talk in the men's hale is not true."

Lani coughed, pretending to clear her throat. Kekoa had never used her full name before. The carefree afternoon had changed, the tone in his voice was like a cloud threatening to cover the sun. "What talk?" she asked, dreading his response.

"They say you are leaving on the voyaging canoe, to join Ikaika and the others."

Her heart began to beat against her ribs. Kekoa must hear the pounding, or at least see the ripples pulsing across the water from where she sat. She should have spoken to him about the trip before he heard gossip from the villagers. Too late now.

"Yes, their talk is true." The Ho'ololi crew were leaving family and friends behind. New friendships forged during the journey would eventually grow into marriages that would carry their new village into the future. "When the wind changes to carry us north," Lani hesitated as Kekoa's face hardened, "the Ho'ololi will sail."

"And you are going?" His tone sliced like saw grass, followed by a stabbing glare.

Kekoa had never spoken to her in anger before. She took a deep breath before continuing. "I will be aboard. The island we seek and Hina's star song are my father's vision, a part of him as much as I am. Besides, the *kūpuna*, the elders who make decisions, picked me as a carrier of my mother's lineage, so I must go."

"You can't!" Kekoa slapped the water violently. The noise startled the birds from the bushes. Squawking, they took flight, their wings flapping against the leafy undergrowth. Before the echo of his shout called back from the valley cliffs, Kekoa had jumped from the pool and stormed away, leaving Lani alone with the petals.

*   *   *

A rush of emotions overwhelmed Kekoa. Lani would soon sail away. The island without her would be like holding the empty husk of a niu, the white meat and the milk, the sweetness and nourishment, would be gone. Ka'imi's vision, the building of the canoe by the village craftsmen, even the choice of who would join the crew, Kekoa knew these events were all part of the natural order of their lives. The voyage was meant to happen. For him to resist or rebel was not right. His tantrum at the waterfall was childish. An embarrassment. He needed to apologize, to make things pono between them before the day ended. He set out in search of Lani and found her in front of the women's hale with the *wāhine*. Unashamed to speak to Lani in front of the other women, he coughed to gain her attention.

"I'm sorry I shouted at you, Lani. I was angry because I don't want to lose you, and I understand the *kūpuna* have decided who will sail on the Ho'ololi. The selecting is done. I stay and you go."

Lani's cheeks burned as the aunties hid toothy smiles behind their hands and tittered. She jumped up before Kekoa could say more.

"Let's walk to the beach where we can talk." She took his hand and led him away from the *hale*.

They made their way down the path to a huge tree, one that grew at the high tide line and had survived many storms. A low branch reached out across the sand. The bark gleamed, polished by the skin of countless couples who had sat there side-by-side. As the moon slid across the sky they remembered fun times together, pranks they had pulled without being caught and adventures they had survived. Long into the night they talked without mention of the canoe or the voyage.

"Lani, tell me about the rest of the Ho'ololi crew." Kekoa dreaded the answer, but he wanted to know who Lani would be with.

"The *ali'i* selected me. I didn't ask to go."

"I know all about the choosing." Kekoa kept jealousy from souring his voice. "How many are sailing?"

"A crew of twelve."

"Are you the only girl?"

"No, there are nine *kāne*, including my father, and three *wāhine*, counting me."

"Who are the other women?"

"One is Lapa'au, a young medicine woman from a neighboring village. Her husband and two brothers were harvesting seaweed from the rocks at low tide. A huge wave took the men by surprise and swept them away. Lapa'au's home holds too much sadness. She's the only one who asked to join the crew. The new village will need a healer with her skills and knowledge of plants, so the *ali'i* were eager to accept her." Lani paused.

"The other is Miki." Lani was reluctant to speak of a woman she did not trust. "I know her from canoe races and trading trips. She is very powerful on the water. That might be one reason she is allowed to be a student of Kele, the master navigator. He selected four of his best students to join him. They will learn how to guide the canoe across the ocean, far beyond sight of any land."

"And who are the men?"

"Well out of the nine, I have named my father and Kele. That leaves Ikaika, he will be our captain." Lani paused. Kekoa coughed like he had sucked in a bug and she waited for him to clear his throat before she continued. "There are two captains of the watch, Maloka and a man I don't know from a village on the windward side. Three of Kele's students, you know those boys from the beach, and Mākaukau, the cook."

"Well, that explains the talk in the *hale*."

Lani ignored his remark and asked, "My turn, Kekoa. Can you tell me about the blue-black water, the deep ocean? Why you don't paddle on trading trips or swim out to the diving rock?"

"I don't like to talk about me and the ocean."

"I need to know. Everyone says you were landed by a fisherman, and that you have no blood kin."

"Both true. I was young, maybe four or five, when I sailed from my home island with my parents."

Lani knew his fear of the deep water wasn't the only reason he was not sailing on the Hoʻololi. His lack of lineage also held him back. Lani had always wondered about his relationship with the water, so she prodded for more. "What happened?"

"Our voyaging canoe sailed from an island far away, following the stars to this cluster of islands. The crew were four young families. We almost made landfall before a powerful storm swept over us. You know the diving rock out beyond the reef? We crashed into it that night. Waves broke the canoe and threw people in all directions. Somehow I came down on a narrow ledge. I clung to the rock like *heʻe*, the octopus. Everyone else was in the water, calling out for their loved ones. I remember their voices in the darkness, especially my mother and father. One-by-one their shouts disappeared until I was alone."

"Who saved you?"

"A fisherman heard me howling the next day. He had to pry me from the rock, like he was pulling me from my parents' arms. He is the one who gave me the name Kekoa. He said I was courageous to hang on."

"So that night still haunts you."

"They were my *ʻohana*, Lani, not only my parents, but my aunties and uncles, my playmates. All of them died out there." Crushed under the burden of a sadness pulled from his past, Kekoa drew a long breath before exposing the source of his fear.

"You've heard stories about the monsters in the deep blue, spirits with no love for those trekking across the ocean surface. I believe the others who were lost didn't just drown or slip below the surface from exhaustion. They were pulled under. I was the only one to survive. That demon is lurking out there, still looking for me because I'm the only one who cheated him that night."

Lani watched a wedge of light twinkle across the water as the moon left the sky. She tried to see the ocean through Kekoa's eyes, but she had never cheated a demon. She rubbed both arms to get rid of the chicken skin. The closest she could come to imagining his fear was from a brief moment years ago when she was fishing with Ka'imi. *Manō*, a big shark, thumped their canoe almost spilling her out. Ka'imi said the nudge was just a warning. "*Manō's* way to tell us, it's time to stop fishing." The big sharks that glided below in the deep water made Lani wary, but not terrified. If she encountered a man-eating beast she might feel different, and that was one reason she never thought about monsters when she swam out beyond the reef.

"You would be safe on the big canoe, Kekoa, and there's room for one more person," Lani insisted. "The *kūpuna* might let you join the Ho'ololi."

"Lani, I pleaded to speak before the *kūpuna*. I was so nervous. When I tried to ask them if I could join the crew, my mouth gaped open like a fish out of water. No words came out. Oh, they had a good laugh. One old one said I should come back when I could live up to my name. 'Show some courage, young man.' Another shook his fist. 'Go away foolish boy. You don't even have a name.' They both spoke the truth."

"Those were cruel words, for him to say you have no family," Lani said. "I wonder..." She lingered on that word, but Kekoa had nothing more to say.

"Well, let's get together tomorrow." She wanted to change the mood before she left him. "I found a bird nest up on the grassy flat I want to show you, okay?" She leaned over and hugged Kekoa tight before hopping down from their perch and heading back to the village. Lani glanced over her shoulder, aware that something besides Kekoa was traveling the path tonight. She started to trot, moving as fast as she could in the darkness back to the *hale*.

Hāmākua Coast

"But you can't stop the story now, Aunty," I protest. "How could Lani just walk away? Is Kekoa following her?"

"Well Meli, I believe Kekoa and Lani were done talking for the night, and so am I." Aunty Min hoists herself up from her chair. "Sometimes you just have to let your thoughts settle. Look honey, the stars are out. Come on now," the screen door screeches as she pulls on the handle and waits for me. A bird in the banana grove answers the call of the door. "Let's go see what the girls have fixed up for dinner. You need to eat and then off to bed."

"Yeah, but..." As I unfold my legs, pins and needles prick my feet. "Ouch!" I sit, slapping my legs back to life, and wonder about love. Will Lani be able to tell Kekoa her true feelings? I think about the boys I know. The only one like Kekoa is much older than me. Why do people fall in love? Does Ka'imi know other spirits that might help Lani and Kekoa? How can the beginning of Aunty's story leave me with this many questions?

"Why do I need to go to sleep early?"

"Uncle Kō and your cousin Lopaka will be here tomorrow, long before first light. If you want to go fishing, you had better be ready."

My heart races at the news of a fishing trip with Uncle Kō. I stand, shaking one leg and then the other before stepping through the door into the warm yellow glow of the bare kitchen light bulb. The table is already set. Steam rises from bowls of sweet potato and pit-roasted pork. Their aromas invite me to my chair. I slide in and reach for the stack of spring rolls. But before my finger-tips touch the platter, an arm snakes out and plump fingers slap me on the hand.

"Where are your manners, Meli?" the youngest aunty, Līhau, scolds, "Wait until someone says the grace."

"Sorry." I fold my hands and press my lips together, hoping she won't call on me because all I can think of right now is the funny dinner table prayer my cousin, Lopaka, taught me when the Aunties were out of the kitchen. "Lord, we thank you for the figs and for the sea, for the garden and for the trees. Help us not to eat like pigs, or we'll offend those who bought the groceries. Amen."

God probably doesn't mind when we tell jokes, but the Aunties would, especially at the dinner table. So I wear my serious face just in case. Lucky for me Aunty Min offers to say the grace.

"Oh dear Lord, we thank you for the feast you have provided. Bless the humble cooks who have brought these plates to our table. Help us to remember people who do not have food on their tables and those who suffer misfortune. Bless our souls to your service."

"Amen" we all say together. As the platter is passed down the table my worries for the suffering masses give in to my growling tummy. I seize a crispy roll, sink my teeth through the wrapping, and suck out the savory tidbits of pork, ginger, and other goodies.

Waking up early is easy when a day of fishing with Uncle Kō beckons. I might even be awake before the rest of the house. I dress in the dark and tiptoe toward the kitchen. Light shines from under the door. I push gently and peek in. Uncle Kō and Lopaka are already at the kitchen table.

Cousin Lopaka reaches around for me from the end of the table, "Ha, Meli! I was just wondering if you gonna be ready in time." I give him a quick hug, then rush around to Uncle Kō. He is so big, when I give him a hug my hands only reach to under his arms. "Uncle Kō, how are you?"

With my cheek pressed against his broad back I breathe in through my nose. Uncle Kō has a distinctive, and to me, pleasant odor. A faint but unmistakable whiff of diesel always clings to his clothes and this morning the scent mixes with the breakfast noodles cooking in the kitchen. The pungent oily smell of diesel always reminds me of Uncle Kō's boat and fishing trips. Good times.

"Aloha Meli, great to see you. Sit right here next to me, and eat quick so we can leave soon."

"Where are you fishing today, Kō?" Aunty Min asks as she ladles a small bowl of noodles and steamed fish from a pot on the stove. Lopaka slides the bowl across the checkered oilcloth to me and I begin to slurp my noodles as Uncle answers.

"Not too far, Min, but we gotta drive all the way over to Hilo. A few miles north of the harbor there's a cove Sam's been talking about. Not going for deep water fish, so I think we'll paddle. Sam is already over there visiting his brother. He'll meet us at the canoe sheds, take their outrigger. His youngest girl, Kiana, is joining us. I think Meli knows her from school."

A day fishing with Uncle Kō and Lopaka is exciting enough, but now that I hear we are going in the canoe I rush my empty bowl over to the counter and the spoon clatters into the sink. I give Aunty Min a hug. "See you tonight. Let's go." I'm at the door expecting to find Lopaka and Uncle Kō right behind me.

"Not so fast," Aunty Min says, stopping me in my tracks. She crosses her arms for one more question. "How late you gonna be, Kō?"

"Don't worry, Min, we'll be home in time for a late dinner. Be ready to fry up some fish."

"Oh, I will." The tea kettle whistles for her attention. A cloud of steam rises as she pours the boiling water through a bamboo strainer. Fragrant tea gurgles into a tall thermos. She gives the stopper a final twist and holds it out to him.

"Thanks, Min, you're the best," Uncle Kō says, tucking the thermos under his arm.

"Of course I am. Now, Lopaka, don't you forget to grab that basket. I packed up a lunch, and that extra thermos next to the stove is for you." She circles Lopaka like a fussy chicken, expecting something to land on the floor any minute. He manages to balance a butter roll on the top of the thermos while leaning over for the picnic basket. I am still holding the door, relieved that at least Uncle Kō is heading for the truck.

"See you later, Aunty," Lopaka says, then he pauses. Eager to be on our way I almost blurt, "Let's go." Instead, since I only mouthed the words, I can overhear him whisper, "We'll talk more about the news from Honolulu after dinner tonight."

Lopaka is finally out of the kitchen. I resist asking him who was doing what in Honolulu. Right now, my nosy curiosity would only cause more delays.

The drive along the Mamalahoa Highway from our town to the bay at Hilo has sharp curves and narrow bridges. Lopaka fiddles with the knob on the radio, but nothing comes in clear except the church hymn station, so he clicks the switch off and leans against the window. I must have snoozed the whole drive to Hilo because I awaken to Lopaka nudging me off his shoulder. From the twinkling lights I recognize we are at the edge of town. Uncle Kō's old blue Ford is the only truck on the road. We drive by darkened store windows, drab and lonely compared to how I usually see them when I come to town with Aunty Min. In a few hours shoppers dressed in bright colors will fill the sidewalks and cars will honk and bustle along the waterfront. Uncle Kō parks his truck along the road. The canoe sheds are silhouetted against a pearly sky glowing in the east. They stand like sentinels, side-by-side on the beach, guarding the boats. In the distance a squall moves across the bay. The surface of the water bubbles with the raindrops.

"Sam and Kiana are sitting under that tree. I'll go down to the shed and get the canoe ready." Lopaka sets the hamper on my lap, slides out, and slams the door. The basket is heavy, but Uncle Kō lifts it over the steering wheel with only one hand and reaches for my hand with the other. I don't think he realizes how short my legs are, or he forgets how high his truck stands off the ground. As he pulls me out the door I scramble to find the running board, and balance there for a second before hopping down to the ground.

"You're the only one with a free hand Meli, give that door a good shove will you?" I slam it hard just like Lopaka. The metallic thump booms like a drum. We walk through the rain toward Sam and Kiana.

I know Kiana from the playground at school. She's a teacher's helper, and even though she's the tallest girl in class she still plays with all the *keiki* during recess. Some of the older kids act like they're better than the rest of us because at the end of next week they will graduate and be out of school forever. Instead of playing games like they used to, they gather in tight circles and talk about moving to the city and looking for work. Kiana is different. She doesn't ignore the little ones.

"Hey Meli, you're up early today, yeah?" Kiana slides from the box. "Aloha, Uncle Kō," she greets him as she reaches for the basket, "Did Aunty Min make us lunch?"

"Aloha Kiana," Uncle Kō says. He and Sam slap hands. Each picks up an end of the wooden box and are on their way to the sheds.

I answer for Uncle. "Yes, she packed tins with spring rolls and butter rolls, dried *he'e*, and a thermos of tea. What's in that box, Kiana?"

"Ice wrapped in seaweed for the fish we catch today. They'll be fresh when you get home. I can't believe my Uncle has a refrigerator. He makes ice right in his kitchen! Come on Meli." She holds out her hand for me and we run to catch up.

Uncle Kō has a big fishing boat with a crew, and sometimes he takes passengers. He is gone for weeks, even months, traveling between all the islands, stopping along the way to sell his catch at harbors near the cities. But if we're cove fishing he would rather paddle. An outrigger canoe is not a small boat. Sam's canoe can hold six people and has two *ama*, the outrigger floats. One side has a plank seat lashed to the outrigger booms, the *'iako*. The other side has a woven net between the *'iako*. Sometimes we rig lines to raise a mast and a faded red triangle sail, but today is calm and we'll paddle. The canoe is heavy. I stay out of the way while they tip the hull and set the rollers. They push the boat down to the water's edge. Once the prow floats in the shallows, I climb in to take my place in the middle seat. To launch, Sam and Uncle Kō stand behind the stern booms with Lopaka and Kiana behind the front outrigger booms. On a count of three they all lift up and heave on the *'iako*. The canoe lurches forward and I hang on. When they are thigh deep in the water the hull lifts, everyone jumps into their seats and grabs their paddles. This is not a race. We're the only boat in the water, but just for fun they all hold their blades poised to dig in. Uncle Kō shouts "*Huki!*" and out we go with a cheer.

Uncle Kō is the steersman, the one in charge. He sits at the stern. Sam is in front of him. I'm in the middle. Kiana is in front of me and Lopaka is at the bow. They paddle together, Lopaka and Sam with their blade on one side, Kiana and Uncle Kō on the other, and with a single word from Uncle Kō they switch sides without missing a beat. To speed through the water a canoe crew paddles in unison and the pace is set by the weakest paddler. Uncle Kō is serious about tying up in the cove before the sun shines over the cliff. Since I am still clumsy on switching sides and would slow them down, my paddle is tucked under my seat. I envy Kiana's graceful paddling. Her paddle slips through one hand as she passes the blade in front of her. Somehow she grabs the bottom of the shaft with the other hand and drives the blade down into the water, all without missing a beat. I brace myself with a hand on each *mo'o*, the edge of the hull, mesmerized by Kiana and Lopaka's backs as they twist and reach, their paddles flashing on opposite sides of the canoe. They work together like they are dancing. Kiana sets the pace and Lopaka balances her stroke.

Kiana starts to sing a paddling song, matching the rhythm as they dip and swing. The men join in on the chorus. *"Hoe aku i ka wa'a."* Do your share, keep going, together we paddle ahead the canoe.

We paddle away from the harbor. The sandy beach in front of the canoe shed shrinks to a pale line before disappearing. Out past the stone breakwater the coast opens up on both sides and we turn to the west. The island looks different from out here. She is no longer individual trees and rocks and waterfalls. The forests and the mountain become a single living spirit; land, rising from the water. I pretend I am with Lani and her friends, traveling to a nearby island. How small we are on this big ocean.

By mid-morning Uncle Kō guides us through a break in the reef and we glide toward the center of the sheltered cove. He peers over the side of the canoe, waiting to drop the weighted line at just the right moment to snag a rock. We are anchored and ready.

Uncle Kō has another plan. "My stomach says breakfast was a long time ago, and why be in a hurry. Let's see what Min packed in that basket Sam, before the growling scares off the fish." He's right and my stomach agrees.

Once the last crumbs are brushed into the water Kiana and I slide over the edge, careful not to splash. We haul ourselves onto the *ama* and sit on the plank. Our weight on this side of the canoe balances Lopaka as he settles into the webbing on the other side. From their seats in the hull Sam and Uncle Kō begin to pull in fish.

"How long has he been back from O'ahu?" Kiana is whispering to me, but she is watching Lopaka leaning down to slide a fish into a net bag hanging off the *'iako*.

"My Uncle Kō? I don't know."

"No silly," she nudges me in the ribs with her elbow, "Lopaka."

"Oh. Just a few days." I wonder why she's curious. "He worked on a pilot boat in Honolulu Harbor, but now he's with Uncle until the end of summer. Why are we whispering?"

A swell lifts the bow, and since I am not paying attention I lose my balance and tumble into the water with a squeal.

"What are you girls screeching about?" Lopaka says, grinning as Kiana hauls me back up onto the plank.

"Nothing," Kiana giggles.

"Don't you go scaring the fish."

"Of course not. Hey Lopaka…" Kiana tries to hold his attention, but Sam and Uncle Kō are keeping him too busy. She leans into me and sighs. "He sure is cute."

I don't know what to say. Lopaka has always looked like family to me. Then I think of my new friend Loloa and his curly hair. Both of these boys have a little bit of Uncle Kō in their nose and chin, and a little bit of Aunty Min in their eyes. But Lopaka is tall and lean with straight hair, while Loloa is short and stout. I decide that my cousin and my new friend Loloa are both cute, each in his own way. Kiana must think I'm old enough to talk about boys, so I venture a timid reply. "I guess so."

Encouraged, Kiana leans in. "You know he is." She glances over to Lopaka who is wrestling with a fish at the end of Sam's line, then whispers in my ear. "Does he have a girlfriend?" She leans back before continuing, "Have you ever heard of the green-eyed monster? Because if he does, even though I know it's wrong, I want what she has."

I'm not exactly sure what Kiana is talking about. A dragon, or does Lopaka's girlfriend have strange eyes? A quiver stirs in my spine at the newness of this 'girl-talk' with Kiana. I hear confusing conversations like this when I eavesdrop in the kitchen during grown-up parties. Unsure of what to say, I repeat something I overheard a woman chirp once. It doesn't make sense to me, but I say the words anyway.

"Kiana, he must be twice your age." I didn't mean to be rude, but Kiana is obviously startled.

"Meli, why would you say that? I'm almost 17. Lopaka isn't that much older than me."

"Then, why would you be worried about, you know, the monster?" I hope Kiana thinks I still understand what she is talking about.

"I've grown up since Lopaka saw me last summer. He could take me to the movies. If I knew more about his girlfriend maybe I'd do something different. A new dress, or do my hair. You know, so I could catch his eye. I feel like he hardly looks at me, at least not like a girlfriend."

"Maybe I could ask him, but only if you want me to. There might be a girl there. Not on the boat, I mean living in town." I want to impress Kiana even though I know I'm about to share something he said to Aunty Min, not to me. "He said he has news from Honolulu."

"Really? You'd do that for me?"

I regret my impulsive offer, but words have a way of tumbling out of my mouth. I remember how I made the same mistake when I first met Loloa, blurting whatever came to mind while he spoke with care. Why couldn't I do the same? I had just promised to nose into Lopaka's business for Kiana. If he found out, I could create bad feelings between us. What was I getting myself into, and was there some way I could back out before it was too late?

"I have enough to share with our friends. You are the last one." Uncle Kō's words snap me back from my worries. Uncle is eye-to-eye with a parrot-faced ruddy brown fish. He hands her to Lopaka, the last *uhu* of the day wriggles into his net bag.

"We can fish again tomorrow, Kō," Sam laughs.

Relieved to set the problem of boys aside, I drop off the plank and splash to the hull of the canoe.

"Can I paddle on the way back?" I ask as I haul myself in.

"For a while. I'll let you know when to rest," Uncle Kō says.

Excited to work with the others, I manage to keep the pace until we clear the shelter of the small bay. The choppy ocean slows me down and Uncle Kō calls out to me. I slip my blade under the seat. Unlike Uncle Kō's big fishing boat there is nowhere to take a nap in a *wa'a*, so I hold the mo'o on each side and close my eyes. Every once in a while a wave comes crosswise and slaps the side of the canoe. Cold water splashes over my lap and wakes me up. If the wave is big enough I reach under my seat and feel for the cord attached to a tin can. I bail out the water and doze until the next wave jumps in.

Once we enter the calm waters of the harbor, Lopaka slows the pace and Uncle Kō calls for me to paddle in with them. We glide across the bay and turn at the last moment, so my back is to the beach. I stay in my seat while everyone else jumps out to push as a little wave lifts the hull. With a grating sound the canoe comes to rest on dry sand. Lopaka runs up to the shed and returns with a metal bucket in each hand, and a slab of wood and a bundle of wet burlap under his arm.

"Hey girls, help me out over here," he says as he wades out and unties the net bags from the canoe. I steady the bucket as Kiana lifts the first bag. A variety of today's catch, some thin and silvery, others plump and red, slide in and quickly fill the bucket with a plop. Next we unroll the burlap. Inside are cool green banana leaves and a skinny sharp knife. Lopaka slaps a fish on the board and slices the belly open. The guts slide into the empty bucket, and he hands the cleaned fish to Kiana. She wraps it in a leaf and I stack the leaf packages on a piece of burlap. While we work off to the side, some men loafing in the shade of the trees come down to help Uncle Kō and Sam heave the canoe back up to the canoe shed. Once all the fish are wrapped, Lopaka and Kiana lift the burlap and carry it between them. Lopaka hands out bundles of fish to the men who helped with the canoe and packs what is left over in the wood box. While they stand around talking, I start kicking about in the sand.

"Meli, clean those buckets and the board. Scrub them up good." Uncle Kō hollers down to me.

I'm not finding any pretty shells anyway, and I'd rather be busy down here than listen to more grown-up talk. I wade out and swirl the buckets, tossing the dirty water as far as I can into the bay. I set them where the water won't tip them over and rub the inside with a handful of wet sand until they shine. I rinse the sand out and set both pails upside down before washing the board. As I squat near the waterline a shadow darkens the sand in front of me. A woman's foot presses down on the edge of the cutting board. Her toenails are packed with dirt and her feet stink like the harbor mud at low tide. Filthy shins disappear under the tattered hem of a greasy dress. Tangled hair hangs over her face.

Although I am startled by her appearance, a kind word is the proper way to speak to a stranger. "We were lucky today," I stammer. "There were many fish, would you like some?"

She mutters while scratching at her forearms with long fingernails. Glaring at the sky, she stomps and begins spitting out sentences. I don't understand a word she is saying. In the middle of her rant I hear my name. For some reason this woman is mad at me! She brushes the hair away from her face and for a moment I wonder why she is crying, until I see that her tears are tattoos. I want to run, but her foot still pins down my board. As I try to wrestle it free, I hear a familiar voice.

"*Hūi*, Meli. '*Ea*, what's goin' on?" Loloa is walking toward us along the waterline, waving and grinning. The woman with the tears takes one look at him, jumps past me, and runs down the beach.

"Loloa, where did you come from?" I hug the gritty cutting board to my chest.

"From da trees. See you workin' by da water. What ya doin'?"

"Cleaning pails." I point to the bay with the board. "We went out early."

"Who dat lady with da heavy foot?"

"I never saw her before. All I did was ask if she wanted a fish, and she got mad. I couldn't understand a word she said. Except my name. How would she know my name, Loloa?"

"Don't know. Dat woman Pukikī," he said, sitting down.

"You mean Portuguese?" I set the board on one of the buckets and brush the sand off the front of my shirt. "Do you think that's where she's from?"

"Yeah. Portagee, yeah. Sound like dat to me." Loloa pats the sand next to him.

As I sit, I notice he looks different, more boyish than when we first met. "Why was she so angry?"

"Don't know for sure, Meli. Some people get twisted in da brain. Maybe dey want what dey can't have, make 'em go crazy."

"Did you see her face? I've never seen a tattoo like that before."

"Sadness comes, yeah, but best to let go. Da marks not goin' away, da tears gonna last."

"She kept hissing and spitting. I think she was about to slap me. You saved me, Loloa."

"Yeah, I do dat for you. Listen, you steer clear of dat lady, okay?" Loloa gives me a hug.

"I will." Thrilled that his arm stays draped over my shoulder, I linger under his casual embrace. I hope Kiana is watching. She might think I have a boyfriend, and tell me all kinds of things Aunty Min never talks about. Maybe Loloa isn't that much older than me after all. Certainly not twice my age. Thinking of Kiana, I laugh out loud.

"What's funny?"

"Oh, nothing. Do you want to go with us, next time Uncle takes me fishing?"

"Aw, naw, not me. Don't like goin' on da ocean, Meli."

"Then how do you catch your fish?"

"From da rocks." Loloa jumps up and his arms fly in an arc. With a little imagination we're no longer on the beach at the canoe sheds.

We're on a rocky coast. His round net sails with a splash into the surf. "Catch plenty fish dat way," his voice brings me back to the sand. I blush as he flexes first one arm, then the other. "Ha, plenty strong, throw dat net all day. Don't need a paddle," he laughs.

"Where are you going next?" Now he looks older, and I'm too shy to ask when I will see him again.

"Don't know, Meli. You be good." He brushes the sand off his backside. "I gonna see where dat lady headin' off."

By the time I gather the buckets Loloa is already halfway down the beach. I run up to the canoe shed and pull on Uncle Kō's shirt. I want to tell him what happened, so he can see the tattooed woman before she disappears. Uncle Kō takes my hand, but ignores me until Sam finishes a story about a big *he'e*, an octopus, he caught last week.

"What, Meli?" When Uncle Kō finally looks to where I am pointing, the beach is empty. Both the lady and Loloa are gone.

"There was a woman, down by the water." I tug him away from the shed so we can look up and down the beach. I don't want the others to hear us.

"I don't see anyone. Why are you so upset?"

I hesitate before telling him, and I leave out the part about Loloa. "A woman stomped on our fish board. I don't know what she wanted, I couldn't understand her. Honest, I didn't do anything to make her mad. I even offered her an *uhu*, but she wouldn't accept. And she had tattoos on her face."

"Maybe she's from a southern island and you just didn't understand her language."

"No, they weren't that kind of tattoo. She had tears." I draw my finger down my cheek.

Uncle Kō frowned and knelt in the sand next to me. "Only a troubled person marks herself so others will always see her pain. That crazy woman is gone now, so you don't need to worry. Let's go home, Meli."

On our way back to the truck I walk in front of Sam and Uncle Kō. Above their banter, I catch fragments of another conversation behind them. Kiana and Lopaka are carrying the wood box between them. I can tell from the tone of her voice she is flirting with him. She pauses between each chirped question.

"Are you home for a while? Really? Here in Hilo? With friends? Do you like the movies? Maybe I'll see you soon?"

Lopaka is not biting. His answers consist of just one word. "Yep."

All I carry is the empty picnic basket, but my feet drag by the time we reach the truck. Uncle Kō doesn't wait for me to climb up onto the running board. He swings me up to the bench seat behind the steering wheel, and I scoot over to my place in the middle.

"Thanks for a good morning, Kō." Sam says holding on to Kiana by the wrist. She is leaning around the front fender, her moon face fixed on Lopaka. He ignores her and clunks around in the back of the truck.

"Always have fun with you, Sam. You two need a ride?"

"No, we're at my brother's for the weekend, Kō. We'll walk from here, it's not far. You keep that ice box 'til next time."

"Then take this with you now for your family, Sam." Uncle Kō digs around in the box for Sam's burlap wrapped bundle. "We should go out again soon," he says as he swings the box up to Lopaka. "I'll let you know, end of the week maybe."

With the box secured in the truck bed, Lopaka jumps over the side and slides into the seat next to me. The passenger door slams shut with a boom. Kiana is still leaning toward the cab at the end of her father's arm.

"Aloha, see you all soon." Kiana sings out.

"Yep," Lopaka grunts. Uncle Kō begins to chortle. As we drive away Lopaka joins in the laughter. I don't understand their joke, and I'm too tired to ask.

*   *   *

I've been waiting for this morning. It's the last week of school before summer vacation. I sit backwards at the kitchen table and hug the rails of the high-backed chair as I watch Aunty bustle about the kitchen. A sack of flour from the pantry, some eggs from the ice box, a little water, and in no time a satin dough is rolled out on the counter. Chop, chop, chop, and fat noodles drop into the pot just as the broth begins to boil. All I have mastered in the kitchen so far are jelly sandwiches, and they aren't pretty. Maybe I need to pay attention. Not just at school, but I should listen to the people in my life. Like Loloa. What lessons will he teach me? My daydream is interrupted by Aunty Min.

"Meli, I'm going into Hilo with Uncle Kō today," she says as she peers into the pot bubbling on the stove. She gives the noodles a stir and turns off the burner.

"Will you be back early enough to tell more of Pueo's story?"

"No, Honey Bee. Anyway, no long stories on school nights." She grabs a kitchen towel and pulls a sizzling pan mounded with golden buns from the oven. "Wait until the end of the week, maybe then."

I hear a truck door slam at the same moment she hangs her apron on the hook beside the pantry. That's another thing I'd like to learn. Perfect timing.

"Lopaka will be fixing up some around the place," she says smoothing back a few stray hairs. "I've made breakfast for the two of you." She pecks me on the cheek and tucks a bundle of papers tied with a ribbon under her arm.

"Let's see, do I have everything?" She glances back, her eyebrows knit together, like she remembered something important to share with me. "Be sure Lopaka eats some of those noodles before he fills up on rolls," she says and the door closes behind her.

Lopaka shouts a rhyme at Aunty, but I can't quite catch her reply. Too bad I missed out, because as he swings through the kitchen door he is still laughing.

"That Aunty, she's a sharp one," Lopaka says as he heads straight to the stove and loads up two noodle bowls. I swivel around in my chair as he sets a bowl down for me, then slides onto the bench where Uncle Kō usually sits and starts slurping his noodles. Chin propped in both hands, I study Lopaka's face in a new light. The way Kiana flirted with him the other day makes me wonder if that's how Lani acted around Kekoa. Does Lopaka know Kiana wants to be more than a pal? I'm not even sure where that would lead. What happens next?

"What are you staring at *keiki*?" Lopaka's voice yanks me back to the kitchen.

"Nothing." My cheeks flush. I shake my spoon at him. "You know, just because I'm short doesn't mean I'm *keiki*, Lopaka. I'm a big girl, almost fourteen."

"A big girl wouldn't fall asleep at the table, would she?" He grins, then asks, "Did you listen to any of the talk after dinner last night?"

I must have missed out on Lopaka's news from Honolulu. As much as I want to help Kiana, I'm too embarrassed to ask Lopaka if he has a girlfriend.

"No." I shift my attention to winding a gob of noodles around my spoon. "The last thing I remember is Uncle Kō telling you to clean up the yard for the aunties while they're in town today because you're going fishing for the rest of the week."

"That's right, better get to work." He shoves his chair back. "Hey, aren't you late for school?"

"I will be if you don't stop asking me questions," I say, trying to duck away. I'm too slow and Lopaka knuckles the top of my head.

"Be a big girl at school today," he chuckles as he heads out the door.

If only the whole school year had been as much fun as this last week. Ever since we went fishing in Hilo, Kiana has saved me a spot on the stone wall where the older girls eat their lunch. Today we sit in the shade and share a tin of pineapple chunks coated with scarlet Tajin, a spicy mix of chiles and lime juice. Kiana stopped asking about Honolulu a couple days ago, which is good because I've been too shy to pester Lopaka. She has other questions about him, things that I never paid much attention to. What does he like to eat? Everything! What is his favorite color? Blue.

"Does he ever talk about going out on dates? Does he like movies or dancing? I was trying to find out and all he would say was..."

I cut her off, imitating his deep voice. "Yep."

"Yep." Kiana winks. "Hold still, Meli." She dips her finger into the sticky juice at the bottom of the tin and paints my lips hot ruby red.

"Wait, don't lick it off." She paints her own mouth and strikes a movie star pose. "How do I look?" She pouts and bats her eyes at me.

"Like a baboon butt."

"Where did you get that idea?" She slaps me and giggles as she licks her lips.

"Science class." I work the spicy mess off before anyone sees what we are up to.

"Will I see you after tomorrow, Kiana?"

"Don't be silly, Meli. I'm graduating, not dying. We'll get together at the end of summer."

"Oh." I swallow the quiver in my voice before I ask, "Is that when you're coming back home?" I had hoped Kiana would be in town all summer, to teach me things Aunty Min never talks about.

"No, I have a summer job in Hilo. I'm going to go live at my uncle's for awhile, but I overheard Uncle Kō talking with my dad. You're supposed to come visit me before school starts."

"In Hilo?" The excitement of staying in the big city with Kiana switches my mood like sunshine coming through a cloud. "Oh, I can't wait!"

"Don't tell anybody, Meli. It's supposed to be a surprise. Now we share another secret."

*   *   *

Secrets are not easy to keep, but I manage to hold my tongue and by the end of the week, a trip to the city seems far off in the future, nothing worth talking about. The last day of school finally arrives. Teacher looks up at the clock, closes her book, and tells us to have a great summer just as the noon hour horn blasts in town. In excitement *keiki* dash from their classrooms, eager to be free from buildings and books. I'm swept along and don't stop running until I'm home. The kitchen is empty, so I throw my knapsack into my room and race out to the lānai. I find Aunty Min, exactly as I had the week before.

"Aloha, Aunty Min," I gasp, flopping down on a pile of cushions. "I'm ready to hear more."

A sparkle comes to Aunty Min's eye. "Let's see." Unlike me, she is never in a rush. She sips her tea and watches the pink-bottomed clouds sail across the sky before she says, "Remind me, where did I leave off?"

"Kekoa told Lani about his dread of the open ocean and why he can't join her on the voyaging canoe. I'm not sure, but I think Lani has decided to sail away without him. How could she? Doesn't she love Kekoa?"

"Well, yes, Lani does love Kekoa, but he is not the only person she must think of. She respects her father and will honor what the *kūpuna* have decided is best for her. Perhaps what happens next depends on Kekoa."

Kāulamana's Spell

Kekoa stared after Lani until she faded into the shadows. The urge to run up the trail, beg her to stay with him, was strong. Instead he sat alone in the early morning starlight. Filled with heartache, he slid off the branch and plodded absentmindedly toward the village. At the fork in the trail he hesitated as if mired in thick mud. His feet nudged him to turn, to climb up the mountain path. The rest of his body paid no attention and pushed him forward, down the well traveled route back home. A few steps further he stopped. A nagging sensation tugged at his feet again, like someone was waiting for him on the mountain. As though possessed, Kekoa turned his back on the village and retraced his steps to the seldom used path. Maybe Kāulamana, the one who worked with mystical powers could help.

He was still a *keiki* when Kāulamana lived in their village. She was a woman who was not easily forgotten. Even now, villagers checked over their shoulders before they gossiped about her and the reason she left to live alone on the mountain. Their stories included whispered rumors of consorting with the gods and goddesses. Some praised her magic, they said she could fix love problems. Others accused her of sorcery. She was responsible for the standing stones at the mouth of the bay. Those young lovers had sought her help, and now they were stuck together forever. Forever is a long time, and his chest tightened. Desperate to keep Lani, Kekoa's heart pounded. The hint of dawn's first light filtered down through the trees and pointed the way. He had to consult the hermit woman. Kekoa took his first step toward Kāulamana.

By late in the day Kekoa's pace slowed to a trudge. The path steepened, a barely visible trace weaving between trees and ferns. Somewhere, maybe close by, the powerful sorceress lived in a dark and damp hole with slimy moss, bundles of bark, and strange smells, all hidden by magic. Some spoke of love potions, but most said her spells caused misery. Which of the stories was true? Hopefully not the one about the lovers changed to a pillar of rock. Unsure of whether Kāulamana would help him or destroy him, Kekoa shuddered.

While Kekoa stood frozen by doubt, Kāulamana sat on a point jutting out from the cliff high above him. She sang softly and gazed across the dense canopy of the forest. She didn't see Kekoa. She didn't have to. She sensed his approach, his footsteps on her forest trail. Her feet swung over the cliff edge as the wind showed itself in the tree tops, swaying this way, then that, back and forth. The dancing trees tickled the bottom of her feet while she played with the wind. This made her merry. Her dark eyes twinkled as a melodious laugh rose and bubbled over.

"He-he-heee! I dance with the wind like a bird." Kāulamana ran her fingers through her long hair, her arms reaching out like wings.

Kekoa stopped in his tracks, searching the branches of the trees high above. What kind of bird was that? He didn't recognize the song. More than just the bird's call was unfamiliar. He was lost, no hint of the path could be seen either in front or behind. Pushing through tall ferns, he continued farther up the slope.

"Ha-ha-haaaa, what fun the bird dance will be," she sang as her laughter reeled him in.

There, the bird called again. Chin to the sky, Kekoa squinted to see what flitted high in the trees, but nothing caught his eye. He stepped around a boulder. A dark form loomed through the tree trunks. Hoping he had reached the cave, he scrambled closer, only to find himself at the base of a massive cliff. At the end of the trail and with no way forward, Kekoa slouched against the bottom of the wall.

With his cheek pressed against the coolness of the stone he stared at the slice of sky high above. The cliff was too steep to climb. Tears blurred his vision. Through the haze a hint of a route materialized from the smooth face. Someone had pulled chunks of stone to form a precarious stairway. Up was the only way. He reached for the first handhold as the bird called from above.

"Hoo-hoo-hoooo," Kāulamana laughed one last time and lay back on the rock giggling. Kekoa was hooked.

Kāulamana's home perched on a terrace that jutted out from the mountain slope. She lived in the open sunshine, high above the jungle. Her shelter was not a dark, damp cave. A broad overhang sheltered her few possessions from the daily rains. Bundles of leaves and flowers for medicine and potions hung on sticks wedged into the cracks in the rock. A small hearth smoldered near the center. The mountain came down to meet the shelter's packed earth floor, a protected place where carrying baskets and mats lay piled in a colorful heap. At the lowest spot in the shelter a piece of hollowed bamboo had been driven into a crevice in the rock to draw moisture from the mountain. Plink, plunk, plink, the sweet water dripped into a carved wooden bowl.

Kāulamana's eyebrows arched as Kekoa's hand appeared and clasped the last rock on her cliff ladder. Visitors rarely reached the top. Jumping up, she trotted over to the shelter, returning with a mat, a gourd of cool water, and a bowl of breadfruit. Arranging these on a patch of short grass in the clearing, she smoothed her skirt, patted her hair, and waited. Kekoa crawled over the edge as the sun dropped behind clouds in the west and the first evening star twinkled in the east.

"*Pehea 'oe* — how is your spirit?" Kāulamana asked.

Kekoa stood and brushed the grit from his knees and elbows. "*Maika'i nō*, fine" he replied. He eyed the shadows of the overhang, wondering if they were alone before he walked toward her.

"*Aloha kāua*, may friendship blossom between us. Come." She gestured with an open palm toward the mat, "sit here and tell me what brings you." In a single graceful move she spiraled down next to the food and drink, waiting for Kekoa to do the same. Elbows and knees akimbo, Kekoa settled across from her. Welcomed by her hospitality and awed by her beauty, he lost his shyness.

He started by sharing his deepest secrets; the doomed voyage from a distant island, the loss of his family and *'ohana*, the loneliness of being the only one to survive the journey, and his fear of the deep ocean. He shared memories of growing up in the village, playing with Lani, and the happy days of his childhood they spent together. He lamented over what he had lost. He would never know his lineage. That was the challenge from the *kūpuna* when he asked to sail on the Ho'ololi. Without a family name he was no one. He had never believed that before. He had always had Lani.

"I've always looked out for her. Just when I admitted how much I needed her, she told me she was going to sail away. I love Lani." Saying those words aloud startled Kekoa. How had Kāulamana tricked him into letting his words flow so freely?

"Your heart has opened and your true feelings spill out," she said, as if reading his mind.

"Boys my age are attracted to beauty and strength," he said, embarrassed to reveal more. "That's one reason I tease Lani into chasing me. She thinks she can't catch me, but she could. Sometimes I hide just to watch her go by." He imagined Lani running down the trail, her thick black hair streaming, and blushed, knowing Kāulamana had probably viewed the scene with him. "When she gives up, I sneak closer and listen to her gasping for breath."

"Beauty feeds physical desire, but do you love her spirit?"

"Yes. That's exactly what makes her so different from all the other girls! She cares for people, animals and plants, even the earth. She can tell when someone is troubled or needs help long before they do, and she helps others before she looks after herself."

Even though his face was veiled by the twilight, Kekoa cast his eyes down while he talked about these intimate feelings. When he looked up, Kāulamana's eyes were closed. He'd better make his request before he put her to sleep.

"The *kūpuna* know my fear of the dark-blue ocean has been with me since childhood. They don't expect me to smuggle myself aboard the Ho'ololi. There must be another way for me to follow Lani."

Kāulamana weighed Kekoa's passionate request. Once the answer came to her she stirred, and her dark eyes held his before she spoke.

"Beware Kekoa. What I conjure will lead you both through danger. This spell is not for you alone. Lani will feel the power of this magic at the end of the journey." She continued to stare, never releasing his eyes. "With this I offer you the first of three warnings. You must accept each one before I will consider casting a changing spell.

"I must follow her."

She pondered further and pursed her lips.

"Take care in asking to follow the Ho'ololi and be sure in your heart. The transformation will push you far beyond your current fears.

"I'd cross the ocean to be with Lani."

"You can follow the stars with Lani to the island of Ka'imi's dreams. If you are still in favor with the gods when you arrive, my magic will follow you both, and you will be together. I ask you one last time, Kekoa, is Lani who you truly want?"

Desperate for Kāulamana's help, Kekoa didn't bother to ask how she knew about Ka'imi's vision and the star song, or why she cared so much about Lani's happiness. The only words he heard were that he could follow Lani.

"Yes. Do anything to me, as long as I can be with Lani," Kekoa affirmed for the third time.

Kāulamana smiled. Rising from the mat, she strode into the gathering darkness toward the overhang. She knelt down to blow on a pile of glowing coals. A small fire sprang to life. In the growing flicker of flames she fetched a small cloth bundle from a pile at the back of the overhang. She unrolled the *kapa* on the ground, selected a handful of twigs, and tossed them on the fire. As the flames curled higher, she sang a melodious chant and began to cast her spell.

Pueo Rising

The first birds began to sing with the dawn while one last bright star still hung in the sky. Kekoa stirred from a deep sleep, wakened by Kāulamana's soft chant. From the mat out in the clearing he could see her in the overhang, still feeding the fire. Firelight danced on the rocks above her. Sparks escaped from under the rock ledge and glittered into the sky. His dry mouth tasted foul. He struggled to stand. What concoction had she given him last night, and why was he so light-headed?

Kāulamana stepped away from the hearth carrying a large round wooden bowl. As Kekoa watched her walk toward him, he felt dizzy. The scene before him seemed distorted, and he fought a rising nausea. He blamed his sour stomach on exhaustion plus the bitter potion she had poured down his throat last night. In the dimness of the dawn she appeared taller than he remembered. He blinked, shook his head, and blinked again. She sat on the opposite end of the mat and placed the bowl down between them. It was full to the rim with water.

"Be calm, Pueo," Kāulamana spoke softly as she reclined, coming to rest on her elbow. "Gaze into the bowl. Who do you see?"

Instead of his own face rippling on the water's surface, an owl gazed back with a feathery disc face and large yellow eyes. Was calling him Pueo and this illusion of an owl in the bowl the extent of her magic? How is a bird going to help me?

Sensing his bewilderment, Kāulamana continued gently. "Just like the boy Kekoa, Pueo the owl is fierce in his devotion. This is the spirit you will use to follow Lani."

Sun rays beamed through the clouds in the east as the morning star shimmered a last glint. His breath rasped in short gasps as he remembered last night. Kāulamana had warned him three times, and with each question he had insisted he must be with Lani. The reflection in the bowl was his own face.

"I will sing the *mele* of your future to you one more time." The sky began to spin as Kāulamana's chant described his fate.

"*Aloha kākou, mana aloha*; all of our love binds us and sets this spell in motion. Let change and transformation follow as I call to each of you who will travel with the Hoʻololi. First, I call to you Kekoa. With every sunrise embrace the power of the day and become Lani's protector, Pueo the owl. Strong wings lift you in silent flight. Golden yellow eyes see in awesome detail. Then, as the last glint of fire from the sun disappears over the horizon, your owl form slips away as well. Change back to Kekoa to be with Lani at night on the Hoʻololi. Wrapped in the stars, you are invisible to everyone but Lani. Go to her. Hold her tight so she does not fear you. In the morning, as the sun's disc breaks above the horizon, become Pueo again. Rise and fly. By day follow the canoe and by night reassure Lani of your love. Next, I call out to you, Kaʻimi. Hear me. The power of your visions will open your heart. At first recognize Pueo's spirit as *ʻaumakua*. As time passes, discover him to be Kekoa, the one who truly loves your daughter. Let wisdom guide your words and actions. Last, I will call to you Lani. With the power of your compassion, stay true to your heart, be courageous, and respect your father. But above all, follow your dream. I will be with the three of you always. *Aloha kākou*, may all of our love seal this spell." Kāulamana continued humming while her words roared in his ears.

"Voo hoo" he spoke, startled when the strange noise sprang from his throat.

Throwing his hands out in a gesture of disbelief, Pueo fell over backwards because his arms were now wings, powerful wings that spanned the distance of elbow-to-elbow in his human form. His body was so light he stumbled up and lunged forward. Struggling at the edge of the mat, he searched for his limbs and fell over again. His hands and fingers had disappeared. He thrashed, trying to find which way was up, trapped in a body that wasn't his.

He couldn't feel the wet grass on his skin. Looking to the sky, he spied a tiny bird hovering, its black wings flapping in stark contrast against the billowing clouds. The distance should have made the bird a speck, but what he could see through the owl's eyes, the detail of the tiny creature, was unbelievable. He panicked, his vision blurred, and then everything went black. His cheek pressed against the earth, and his beak snapped at the grass as he hissed.

Kāulamana had thrown a soft *kapa* over Pueo. Holding him gently against the ground with the bark cloth, she whispered.

"Pueo, don't waste all this good magic with fear."

He couldn't help his reaction. His heart raced as he struggled against the kapa. The gentle pressure of Kāulamana's hands would surely crush him and the chattering coming from his throat added to his fright. The sensation of being seized triggered an instinct to continue fighting. Pueo felt helpless. Unable to escape his captor, he became rigid in a state of shock and exhaustion.

"Stop a moment and find yourself Pueo. Wings and feathers are your new body during the day." Kāulamana's voice came to him through the cloth. He could feel the warmth of her hands as she held him. The prospect of changing from boy to owl and back again every day distressed him. He had only himself to blame since he had pleaded for a way to follow Lani.

"Don't worry. In your heart you are always Kekoa, so think of Lani and take a deep breath. Speak to me with your heart."

Memories of Lani came to him; the expression on her face when he apologized in front of the aunties, her soft voice at the beach coaxing him into telling her his secret, the sweet smell of her hair when she gave him a parting hug. Along with the soothing sound of Kāulamana's voice Pueo managed one deep breath and then another. Having no other choice, he accepted the gift of this new body.

Unsure of how to speak with his heart, Pueo kept making strange squeaks and squawks until in exasperation he clamped his beak tight. He focused his mind on one simple emotion, gratitude. "I will honor your gift."

He was surprised by the brightness of the light, and that his intent had been understood. "Good morning Pueo, welcome," Kāulamana said, as she lifted the *kapa*.

Flexing his talons into the grass Pueo stood upright, weaving slightly as he accustomed himself to the way his new legs worked. He ruffled his feathers, folded his wings, and stretched to his full height.

With her elbow on the mat and her head propped in her hand

Kāulamana reclined next to Pueo. Her eyes looked into his.

"Come, exchange breath with me. Always carry in your heart the joy and happiness I wish for you and Lani."

Still unsure of his balance, he took hesitant steps up to her face and closed his eyes. Kāulamana exhaled through her nose. Her breath gently stirred the sensitive feathers on his face as he inhaled. With each shared breath a calmness washed over him.

A baby's first steps are full of mistakes. Pueo's new body was covered with feathers. He yielded to a sudden urge to spread his wings and fly. But flight required more than just a desire to soar and the energetic flapping of wings. After an initial take-off, rising straight up, and a startled pause that resulted in an immediate crash down, one thing was obvious. Pueo did not know how to fly.

"Don't rush. Jump about first and feel the lift from your wings," Kāulamana coached.

He hopped and flapped in the grassy clearing. His wings provided more lift than he expected. Slight changes in the angle of what had been arm bones now directed his flight feathers. Flying was so different from swimming. Soaring was trickier than floating, and gravity made the unexpected happen a lot faster.

"Try to land in the spindly tree, over there," Kāulamana said, pointing toward the overhang.

He took off and flew to the tree with ease, but when he grabbed the branch, he forgot to stop flapping. He somersaulted and fell with a poof of feathers into the bushes. Still determined, he hopped back out into the opening and tried again with similar results. Kāulamana tried to hold in her laughter, but his efforts were too comical. Tears of mirth rolled down her cheeks. He soon coordinated the timing of talons and wings and managed to stop gracefully. The sun glared high above before he mastered taking off and landing. He swooped back and forth in celebration and stopped gracefully at the edge of the mat.

Kāulamana reached for a basket at her side. Holding the loosely woven lid over the opening with one hand, she slid her other hand inside. Pueo watched with curiosity, tilting his head one way, then the other. She flung her hand toward the clearing, and a dark ball sailed out. With animal instinct, Pueo lifted off, swooped low, and snatched up the fluttering shadow, returning to her.

"Lunch time, Pueo," she said as she bit into a juicy yellow fruit. He tore into the ball he held between his talons. The human deep within was momentarily disgusted by the texture of feathers.

"Should roast first." He glared, feeling tricked by her actions.

"You are not hungry?"

"Raw not favorite." He considered the limp dove and resumed plucking feathers. His empty stomach had won the argument.

"Only when you land on the Ho'ololi will you enjoy human food again. Today you need to eat and build your strength, so you can find the canoe. Feathered creatures, lizards, even fat insects will keep you alive. But enough talk, I hear drums. The Ho'ololi sails, and you must follow her."

Kāulamana crossed the clearing and settled on her rocky perch. She dangled her feet as the wind played in the tree tops. Pueo lifted off, hovered a moment, and then arched across the clearing. Brushing her bare shoulder with his wing tip, he rushed beyond the cliff edge toward the sea. The forest fell away, far, far below.

Come Sail Away

L ani awoke to an empty hale. The angular shadows of the bamboo roof poles told her the morning was half gone. Her ears perked to a slight change in the routine of the village, more activity, more chattering, a different pattern to the voices. Night before last she had stayed out with Kekoa almost until dawn. Yesterday she waited for Kekoa late into the night, but he never came to her. She covered her head with her arms, and was drifting off, only to be rudely awakened.

"Hey, lazy girl! Time to go," Miki crowed, jumping with a thump onto the hale platform.

Miki was not the first person Lani wanted to see this morning, but there she stood. She had a hard mouth, a sharp tongue, and was quick to stick her nose into everyone's affairs. Miki had been bragging for weeks now about joining the crew. Her boastful ways made some villagers feel that the canoe couldn't leave soon enough.

"Time to go?" Lani grumbled from under her arms.

"Don't be stupid, girl. The Ho'ololi?"

Lani pushed herself upright as Miki continued.

"The wind changed, the last of the supplies are being stowed, so grab your bags," Miki said as she jumped off the hale platform. "Don't make us wait for you, again," she shouted as she ran down the path toward the beach.

Miki was competitive on land, but was even more aggressive on the water. She would fight for a canoe seat and only paddle with the fastest crews. Lani, who loved to be out on the open water, chose lighthearted crew mates. Having fun seemed more important than being first. Lani seldom paddled on winning canoes, as Miki had just reminded her.

Her last outrigger canoe trip to ʻEiao, a small island nearby, had been an embarrassment. The villagers of ʻEiao quarried a fine-grained rock and shaped them into stone tools. A *koʻi* from ʻEiao was coveted by craftsman on her island for carving wood figures and shaping canoe hulls, so five canoes had paddled over to exchange *kapas*, bark cloth, for the tools they needed. A trading trip isn't a race, but when a group of outriggers paddle together the pace quickens when the second canoe decides to be first, and the first canoe doesn't yield. Lani and her crew fell behind and a change of wind and ocean swells swept them toward the windward side of ʻEiao. Its cliffs curved like the crescent of a new moon, reaching out for them. They worked hard to paddle around the point, but never caught up to the rest of the canoes. The last paddlers to haul onto the trading beach always suffered the teasing of those who landed earlier. Miki had been the first to taunt Lani and her companions.

"Argh," Lani groaned and propped her chin in her hands. Being late was a shameful trait, but here she was, the last one again. Two bulging carry bags sat in the corner, surrounded with little piles of household items. Lani had been repacking them for days. She crawled out of her bed, forced to make the final selections of what to take and what to abandon.

At the base of the center pole of the hale a small adze bound to a polished handle caught Lani's eye. This *koʻi* had been a gift from Kaʻimi after their last trading trip. Lani wondered if anyone else packed one? The blade could reshape a broken beam, or crack a skull if wielded in a warrior's hands. She wrapped the tool in a small mat to protect the sharp edge, tied the bundle with a stout piece of cord, and repacked the contents of her bags one last time. All the delicate supplies, sewing and weaving awls, drinking cups, bowls and spoons, sealed gourds with snacks, pieces of bones and shells wrapped in a fine woven cloth, and the tools for making fishhooks and sinkers, filled one bag. The other bag had the adze at the bottom, followed by weights, raw materials for weaving and repairing lines, fishing lines, topped off with coarsely woven *kapas*.

Looking around one last time a sparkle on the corner post caught her eye. Standing on her tip-toes, Lani retrieved a pendant from a high peg. Kekoa had carved the likeness of a Kolea, a migrating land bird, from a piece of golden shell. The charm hung from a loop of cord made from twisted strips of fibrous leaf. They had exchanged their first kiss when Kekoa slipped the cord over her head. She would always treasure this gift, a keepsake of their love. Rubbing the shell between her thumb and finger she sang a traveler's prayer. Was she like Kolea, a small land bird about to sail a great distance across the ocean? Her song asked for plenty of fair weather, fresh water, and dolphins to grace their journey. Lani sang as she shouldered her carry bags, took one last look around the *hale*, and headed down to the beach.

She arrived in time to see the feast platter lifted aboard the Hoʻololi. In a rush Lani ran to her favorite aunties. Tears filled her eyes as she shared breath with each of them one last time. Kaʻimi reached for her bags, and tossed them over the *moʻo*. The *aliʻi* stood with the crew and amid great ceremony the *kahuna* blessed the *waʻa*, the Hoʻololi. With enormous manpower the whole village helped heave the voyaging canoe the last few yards across the sand. The timing of the launch took advantage of the changing wind and tide. As the stern cleared the white foam on the beach, the drums and farewell chants boomed. Lani looked hard at each person, so she would remember all the faces she would never see again.

Ikaika, the captain, stood at the front rail of the *pola*. The *aliʻi* trusted him to keep the canoe and the crew safe. Everyone aboard had sailed with Ikaika from this bay, but those were short fishing trips with only a few people. The voyage to raise the new island would take weeks, maybe longer. There were twelve aboard the Hoʻololi, a crew of nine men and three women. Setting the pattern for many days to come, Ikaika called orders to the captain of the first watch. The man at the steering paddle adjusted their course toward the gap in the headlands that protected the bay from the open ocean swells. Others worked the rigging lines for the sails. The Hoʻololi sat low in the water. Her *moʻo* kept all but the biggest waves from splashing in. Each hull weighed a ton, packed with food, tools, plants, fresh water, even a family of puaʻa, pigs. The seams were caulked with niu fiber, sealed in place with tree sap. As the *waʻa* lifted with the wind, a celebration on the beach began. Men pounded drums and chanted, and women danced. Food disappeared from platters and more were carried through the crowd with great ceremony, heaped high with fish and fruit. The whole village had gathered to witness their departure, everyone that is, except Kekoa.

Lani leaned over the side board to keep the villagers in view.

"Kekoa, why didn't you come say goodbye?" she whispered to no one. "Surely you hear the drums?" Their thunder carried across the island, echoing off the cliffs. Her sadness grew with the pounding rhythm.

The coolness of a shadow fell on Lani's shoulder. Miki stood between Lani and the sun.

"Did I tell you, Lani, I saw Kekoa heading up to the high cliffs early yesterday?" Miki knew her words added to the doubt that clouded Lani's heart. "He must have been miserable, you know, staying behind, while you sail away with all these men."

Lani refused to answer Miki's hissing.

Miki continued, "I hope he didn't hurt himself up there in the cliffs. What else could keep him from showing up today? Maybe Kekoa made an offering, you know, jumped from the rocks as a gift to the gods."

Lani spun around. "Stop casting a shadow on me, Miki. Your tongue wagging could bring all of us grief." Lani spat before she turned away from Miki and climbed up to a seat at the *manu hope*, the high back end of the hull.

From her perch Lani looked across her floating home. The prospect of living so close to Miki sank in. She vowed silently to avoid her. At least her father always had a kind word to share. When the crew began to stow away their gear, Ka'imi had claimed this hull's hope as a secluded spot for his visions. He had hung a mat and stowed their possessions at the base of the seat. A private place was essential on a crowded vessel. Lani would sleep behind the mat during Ka'imi's watch, and then they would trade places. She swiveled around and sat cross-legged. The beach blurred into the surf, a shrinking line of white far behind. A craftsman had wrapped a thick plaited rope around a narrow grooved part of the *manu*. A *ki'i akua*, a small carved idol, had been secured with a cord to the rope. From high on the mast a *lei hulu*, a woven streamer of feathers, twirled and fluttered above the canoe like a bird following closely. Both the *ki'i* and the *lei* were offered as blessings, to bid the spirits to watch over and protect them. As the feathers danced in the wind, Lani clutched her necklace and sang her prayer to Kolea again. Lani wished her spirit could soar like a bird, back to the island to find Kekoa for one last hug, one last kiss goodbye.

The Ho'ololi glided from the sheltered green waters and passed beyond the rocky arms that embraced the bay. The canoe swung to the north, her sails full with the wind that blew across the open water.

From the ridge pole of a *hale* at the edge of the beach Pueo had watched the celebration of the canoe's departure. He sat unnoticed like a wooden carving. Long after the canoe had sailed around the point, the villagers finished the last of the food and the beach emptied. Pueo lifted off. He swooped along the edge of the forest and up the cliff face toward the north point of the headland. At the precipice he hovered, unwilling to leave the land behind. He could clearly see every detail of the waves as they crashed against the jagged rocks far below. He circled on an updraft as the Ho'ololi shrank to a dot and disappeared. He heard Kāulamana's warning; "far beyond your childhood fears." As the waves beat against the shore, the current dragged the white foam out to sea. The deep dark blue. Earlier he had focused on Lani's face as the Ho'ololi left the island. Holding firmly to that last glimpse of his love, Pueo moved beyond the surf line. Again he hovered, frustrated that the point on the horizon where the canoe had vanished was fading. Only one choice remained. He flew out across the open water.

Eager to join Lani, Pueo kept a steady pace and soon spotted the Ho'ololi. As he approached the canoe, he realized that he hadn't considered what might happen. If an owl landed on their deck before the first nightfall, some of the crew might fear their journey was shadowed by a land spirit. Circling high above, he watched the canoe carve a straight line across the water. Their path, like a spear thrown out toward the horizon, would pass by the northern islands tonight. Kāulamana warned that he would become a boy when the sun set, but she didn't say how that would happen. Even if he landed on the deck and managed to stay hidden, he had no idea at what precise moment the sunset would bring about his transformation from bird to boy, or how long the switch would take. If he screamed out in fright or pain, he would be found out right away. He couldn't risk being discovered, at least not now while they were so close to land. The Ho'ololi could easily change course and put him to shore on 'Eiao. He decided to pick out his own island, spend the night alone, and catch the Ho'ololi tomorrow.

Shining Star

Lani's home disappeared behind the voyaging canoe as the northern group of islands came into view beyond the *manu ihu*, the snout of the opposite hull. As they passed landmarks and observed the journey of the sun toward the horizon, she felt the distance between her and Kekoa growing. By the end of the day the last island of her homeland had sunk into the sea with the sun and along with it so did her heart. Kekoa was gone forever.

In the twilight the boundary of sea and sky was unbroken in all directions, the last glow of day vanishing without a cloud in sight. On other canoe trips clouds had always gathered over distant islands or drifted across the sky, like giant canoes sailing across an ocean high above. This evening was cloudless. The entire bowl of the sky had been turned upside down and more stars than she could count were spilling out. Their light spread a silver glow across the calm ocean. She found small comfort knowing that she still shared these same stars with Kekoa.

Lonely under the vast starry night, Lani sought out the company of Ka'imi. She found him at the stern seat, gazing back toward home.

"Did you eat yet, father?"

"Ah, Lani, my dear. Yes, I had yams and pit roasted pig earlier." He gestured for her to come sit next to him as he asked, "Did you share in the feast, Lani?"

"I did. The village provided us with so much food, but soon the platter will be bare. What are you watching?"

"Today's path slipping over the edge of the world."

Lani stared hard into the darkness. A faint glow from their wake trailed behind. Surely Ka'imi was watching more than a line of foam in the starlight. Looking toward the *manu ihu*, no visible path shone before them. Lani wondered what the ocean looked like to her father. She listened to the quiet voices of the crew and the creak of the lashings as Ho'ololi flexed over the swells. Time slid past while a comfortable silence hung between them. Lani searched to find the right way to express what was in her heart.

"I have never seen the stars like this before, father, pouring over us from the sky. On our island, at night on the beach or in the dark of the forest I know exactly how I fit in, where I belong. But out here, we are so small. I just don't know." Waves rushed along the hull with a soothing hush-hush sound. Lani knew their talk couldn't be rushed. She waited. He sat next to her, but his spirit wandered in the stars.

"We named you Hokulani for a sky like this, all the stars of heaven," Ka'imi said. His eyes left the sea and focused on her face, softly illuminated by the starlight. "The preparations for the voyage have kept me busy. You have grown so much in the last year. I hear the heartbreak of a young woman in your voice. More than just leaving our island burdens you."

Most of the time Ka'imi seemed so distracted. Now he answered the question she hadn't even asked. His words gave her hope.

The motion of the canoe on the open ocean swells, as it glided up-up-up, paused as the hulls slid over the top of the swell, and then down-down-down the other side, reminded Lani of rocking a baby to sleep. Her eyes closed, the creak of the crossbeam's lashings that connected the two hulls and the hum of sail lines sang a comforting lullaby. She was nodding off when Ka'imi spoke again.

"I saw an *'aumakua* follow us long after we sailed past the headland. The bird kept his distance. I could not recognize who the spirit was before he turned away toward 'Eiao. I will search for that guardian in my dreams tonight and share what I find with you tomorrow."

A protector's spirit would be a welcome addition to the crew, but why didn't the bird join them today? Instead of an answer, Ka'imi had just given Lani another mystery to ponder.

* * *

A steady wind filled the sails all night, pushing the canoe many miles to the north. Lani woke before dawn, excited to see the first sunrise at sea. Kele, an experienced guide and way-finding teacher, stood braced against the rail. His students were silhouettes against the backdrop of a golden sky, their hands reached from the horizon to the heavens. Lani moved closer to hear Kele explain how to read the stars.

"The span of your hand, finger-to-thumb, is a tool you always have with you. Use your hands to measure the horizon. Use the canoe, the masts, the *manu hope*, and the *manu ihu*, to mark our position. As the stars move, we will make new readings to keep us on our path."

Kele asked each student to count the sections and quadrants of the horizon. They each named a navigation star, pointing to where it would rise, swinging their arm in an arc that followed its path across the sky, and stopping at the place where the star would set. At home Lani had watched the navigators, drawing in the sand, making patterns of sticks and shells, and singing star songs. On the ocean far from any landmarks wayfinding didn't look like a game anymore. Knowing the heavens and the course they would follow across the sea was a survival skill.

Unlike watching the stars from their island home, a mix of natural forces came together on the open ocean as the Ho'ololi sailed across the water. Winds filled the sails, sending the canoe one way. They also pushed against the hulls, moving her in another. The swells lifted and fell away as invisible currents swept along beneath them. To know the movement of the stars, and factor in the influence of wind and waves on the canoe, the navigator's apprentices needed to master complex calculations in their heads. Kele would ask these questions every day: Where would the guiding stars rise and set? Was there any change in the swells and winds? They had just left their home island; which direction did the birds fly this morning? Which direction would they fly as they approached their destination? How fast were they sailing? What corrections would keep them sailing with Hina's star song?

"The world all around you," Kele said as he made a grand sweeping gesture, "will help you find your way, but the most important wayfinding is within. My question for each of you, can you see Ka'imi's island in your hearts? Your spirit must always be connected to your destination, otherwise you will become lost."

Lani pondered Kele's lesson. She realized that to be in harmony with this journey, she had to make a connection, not only to the island they were sailing toward, but with the people on the Ho'ololi. These men and women were her new family, her *'ohana*.

Lani respected Kele's knowledge and Ikaika's leadership. The men on the steering paddle had muscle power, and those who adjusted the lines made the sails dance with the wind. Kaʻimi held the vision of their destination. Keleʻs students, in addition to being able sailors, were becoming navigators. Lapaʻau had her bundles of plants and potions to keep them healthy. So far, everyone on the canoe had a purpose, except Lani. She needed to be more than just a lineage carrier, an idle girl with no skills. She must find a way to contribute to the voyage, no matter how small the job. Lani noticed that Mākaukau, the cook, was working alone, organizing his kitchen.

"Can I help you, Mākaukau?"

"I always say yes to extra hands, Lani" He grinned as he passed her a board and chopper.

At the end of the early morning watch the crew gathered to share the first meal of the day. Last night's feast had been a farewell gift from the villagers, a wood plank stacked high with roast pig, baked roots, and fruit puddings wrapped in leaves. This meal was simpler, chopped on plank boards, tossed on a platter, and served into each sailor's wooden bowl. Lani helped clean up after breakfast. She was scrubbing at a stubborn stain on the cutting board when Ikaika took her elbow and pulled her aside.

"Lani, I have spent years fishing with Kaʻimi, and so have you. When the *kūpuna* planned this trip they selected Kaʻimi to be our fisherman. This morning he surprised me. He refused the job, because the responsibility would be a distraction. He wants to focus on the island vision and Hina's star song. Although some of the crew might grumble that a girl fishing from a man's boat is forbidden, this is my decision to make, not theirs."

Lani eagerly awaited Ikaika's next words. Although it was forbidden for a girl to sail with men in a fishing canoe, everyone aboard knew of the time long ago when Kaʻimi took her away from the village. Day and night Lani was at her father's side. They had worked together to survive. He had taught her how to shape bone and shell into intricate hooks and lures that fish found irresistible. She had learned his secrets; to judge both how deep the fish swam and which lure they would chase. Years later when they returned to the village, Kaʻimi ignored the *kapu*, what was forbidden, and still invited Lani to go out in his canoe. No one dared stop him.

"Your talent at bringing fish matches his." Ikaika held her eyes with his. "On this voyage you will be in charge of the lures and lines."

Lani was stunned. Only one person was selected to fish on a voyaging canoe. Ikaika had given her both the right, and more importantly, the responsibility. Lani resisted the urge to jump up and down and shout with glee. She swallowed hard to control her voice as she accepted. "Fishing for the Ho'ololi is an honor, Ikaika. Thank you."

Ikaika scowled and leaned in close to whisper. "You'll do fine." His stern voice made his bulk even more imposing. The tension passed as the twinkle in his eyes spread to his lips, and shone on his face. This was the Ikaika Lani knew best, a kind soul who was quick to smile with the smallest pleasure. Declaring her to be the Ho'ololi fisherman was a serious choice, for he tested both Lani and the crew. This respect for her skills made her silently vow to be the best fisherman a voyaging canoe ever had.

Every day she would send the lines studded with lures and hooks off the back of the canoe. With luck and the blessings of the gods, she would haul in the catch and help Mākaukau clean and prepare the fish. Raw or marinated in seasonings, fish would be served at almost every meal. From now on the crew depended on her for fresh food while she relied on their skill to sail the canoe to their new island home. Ho'ololi was her new *'ohana*, a small relief for her broken heart.

Travelers

Pueo had followed the Ho'ololi as she sailed from their island. Hovering high above the canoe, the risk of being discovered aboard on the first day out made him hesitate, and his hunger had made it easier for him to turn away. He flew back to an island north of 'Eiao, circled over a grassy terrace, and began hunting for unwary critters scurrying across the patches of bare ground. He stuffed himself until he could eat no more.

Kāulamana had not offered Pueo any details, she had only warned him to be secure when the sun went down. Leaving himself plenty of time before sunset, he flew north toward the last scrubby isle he could see. When the sun touched the horizon, his transformation from owl to boy was quick and painful. The barbs of his feathers retracted into the quills, and the quills disappeared into his stretching skin, a nauseating sight. As his bones grew, Kekoa ached all over like he was sick with fever.

He should have found a suitable shelter while he still had wings. Kekoa stumbled around in the twilight, gradually adjusting to his weak human eyesight. His body lacked the cover of Pueo's feathers, his feet the protection of scaly talons. He didn't notice he was naked until he sat down to take a thorn from his foot. After his bare bottom scraped the rough rock, he wished for his loin cloth.

As the last glimmer of twilight disappeared, Kekoa discovered two boulders leaning together, sheltering a small wedge of dry sand. He scuffed both knees and elbows as he wormed his way in, glad to be out of the wind. Instead of a deep sleep worry crept out of his heart and roared in his ears. If he couldn't find the Ho'ololi tomorrow, if he were caught over the water when the sun set, he would fall like a rock into the ocean and die! To avoid certain death he would have to judge the time of day and remember exactly how far he had flown from this rock. But he would be flying slower, against the wind, if he had to return. Knowing the halfway point, where to make the decision to turn back to land, would be critical. Yet giving up would mean losing Lani forever. Then he'd be stuck. Half boy, half owl, the rest of his life with no one to love.

"No worries," he shouted into the darkness. The sound of his human voice pushed away the tormenting thoughts and cleared his mind. The only solution was to rest. Tomorrow he would find Lani. Kekoa wriggled his back against the rock, curled into a ball, and endured a fitful sleep.

He was awake before dawn. For a moment Kekoa was sure that he had rolled off his mat onto the stone floor of the men's *hale*. The visit to Kāulamana and the departure of the Hoʻololi seemed a fantastic dream until he sat up and cracked his skull on the low rock ceiling, a rude reminder of his situation. He crawled out from under the rock shelter on hands and knees and sat shivering, not from the cold but in antici-pation. The first rays of the sun found his long bones twisting into short ones. His sprouting feathers jabbed his smooth skin like a thousand thorns. Pueo shook out his wings and launched himself skyward. He played with the push and pull of the wind and dropped lower or flapped higher to stay in the best current. The further north he flew he noticed all the other birds that swept by were seabirds, buoyant if they chose to rest on the swells. For Pueo, flying was the only choice.

Half the day he traveled north over the endless sameness of the water until he spied a piece of island debris adrift, a tree or bundle of palm fronds cast out to sea by storm winds or waves. Not believing his luck, he spiraled down. The wreckage of a hale roof, the thatching mostly gone but the lashing still holding the poles quite tightly, floated below him like a raft. Saddened by the fact that this refuge probably marked the halfway point in his search for the Hoʻololi, Pueo settled silently on the high end for a much needed rest. He closed his eyes and relaxed in the warmth of the mid-day sun. Time to decide. Reluctant to admit defeat, he opened his eyes and was surprised to see Kolea, a golden plover, dozing in a tuft of palm frond at the other corner of the thatch raft. He had heard about these ocean travelers from voyagers' stories. Long ago he had carved a shell, a delicate likeness of Kolea, and given the pendant to Lani. These small birds that migrated vast distances across the ocean were good luck. He stared, wondering how long this bird had been sleeping. As the minutes passed, he became curious. Had Kolea come from the north? Sensing the stare of a predator, the plover's eyes flashed open.

"Hello," Pueo said, "I'm sorry to wake you. I was wondering…"

"Please, don't eat me! I'm small, all feather and bones, no meat, really no meal for you at all." Kolea crouched in fear.

"No, no, don't be afraid." Pueo wasn't considering a snack. Unaware of how menacing he appeared to the small bird, he continued, "I need your help."

Kolea shifted behind the thatch. "My help?"

"Wait," Pueo said, "I'm talking to a bird?"

"Don't you know birds can talk to each other?" Kolea still huddled behind a frond, unsure of what trick the owl might be up to.

"This doesn't make any sense. How can I understand you?"

Kolea sat up, now sure that this Pueo was no ordinary owl. "Well, what doesn't make sense to me is seeing a land bird like you out here."

"I'm new at being a bird, and how I ended up this way is a long story. I was changed into an owl, but the spell only lasts during the day. When the sun sets, I'll be Kekoa again, just a boy."

"A new owl, hatched by magic? That is a curious situation." Weeks had passed since Kolea last heard a good story. "Tell me more."

"I'm trying to find my friend, Lani. She's on a voyaging canoe."

"Has Lani also been changed into an owl?" Kolea worried that another owl, maybe not as friendly as this one, would show up any minute.

"No. I'm sorry to rush, but I don't have time right now." Pueo shifted from foot to foot, flexing his talons nervously, tearing the fronds into ribbons. "I have three choices. None of them holds much promise. If I turn back now, I land safely on an island and lose Lani forever. Or I keep flying north, but if I don't find the canoe by sundown, I'll fall from the sky and probably drown. The third option is to stay here, but I don't think this raft is big enough to hold my human weight tonight, and even if it does, tomorrow I will be even further away from the canoe."

"Oh, so you seek the double-hull canoe." Kolea stared as Pueo continued to shred the thatch. He didn't want to be the owl's next meal and hoped his answer would inspire Pueo to leave right away. "Maybe we're both in luck. I passed a canoe just over the horizon." Kolea gestured north with his thin curved beak. "Fly with the swells in that direction, and you will find them before dark."

"Only if I hurry." A few powerful beats of his wings lifted Pueo high above the raft. He hovered and swooped back. "Thank you Kolea and safe journey."

"You too, Pueo. *Aloha!*"

Pueo sped away across the swells. It was good fortune that Kolea could guide him toward the canoe. He only wished he had remembered to ask when the little bird had seen the Ho'ololi.

Kohala Coast

"Pueo and Kolea shared a blessing for a safe journey, a good place to stop for tonight, Meli."

Until I heard my name I was still flying after the Ho'ololi with Pueo. Disappointed to find myself sitting on the *lānai*, I hope Aunty won't mind a few questions.

"How did Kāulamana know Kekoa would agree to her magic?"

"She didn't, so she chose the spell that would allow the power of his love to soar."

"Did Kekoa realize he would give up half of himself just to follow Lani?"

"No, because he listened to Kāulamana with his heart, not his head."

"Was Ikaika using his heart when he decided to break the rules? I thought in the old days girls weren't supposed to fish."

"He knew the Ho'ololi sailed on an uncharted course for an island that only Ka'imi had seen. A strong leader must take risks, using both his heart and his head. As captain, Ikaika was wise to honor Lani's skills. And Lani became stronger when she accepted his challenge."

For the first time I wonder who might be changing my direction. If life is about making choices, then I guess that also means accepting mistakes. Not just mine, but other people's too. My eyebrows knit together. People must struggle with tough decisions all the time. If you don't make a choice, somebody else will make it for you. Or even worse, you find out you have picked the wrong way.

"Remember Meli, don't be afraid to let go. Apologize, forgive, and move on with your life."

It's spooky when Aunty Min reads my mind. "Okay, I'll try." I jump up to hold the screen door open for her.

"Why thank you, Honey Bee." She squeezes my shoulder and calls out, "Sisters, set an extra place for Lopaka and Kō. These old bones of mine tell me they'll be here for a late dinner."

"How do you know Uncle Kō is coming?" I ask as I follow her into the kitchen. Aunty Min can see a visitor long before the rumble of their truck or clanking of their bicycle announces them coming down our rutted driveway.

"I feel him in my bones. The *mana*, his life energy, speaks to me. One day you will listen and trust what your own bones tell you, Meli."

I hold out my scrawny arms. "Maybe I'm too little?"

"No bones are too small," she chuckles. "Go wash up, Meli. We'll have our dinner now. They'll be awhile."

After dinner I stand on a step-stool at the sink with an aunty on either side. Three sets of hands make quick work. As I pass the last plate to Aunty Līhau, a pin-prick of headlights turn off the highway. "They're here. Just started down the road."

Boots stomp across the *lānai* and the old bench creaks. I help carry the serving dishes from the oven back to the table before the kitchen door opens.

"You look worn out." Aunty Min welcomes Uncle Kō with open arms, "Are those fish making you work too hard?"

"Ah yes, they are Min, but we were blessed. So many fish jumped into our nets that we had to come home early." Uncle Kō pulls the bench up to the table, Lopaka plops into a chair on the other side, and the rest of us gather round. The aunties share village news while Uncle and Lopaka busy their mouths with the food.

"Now, maybe we have some home time, yeah?" Lopaka asks as he leans his chair back on two legs and rubs his hands back and forth across his belly.

"Maybe for a few days, but the harvest at Sakamoto's orchard in Hawi is coming up soon. I offered him your help." Uncle digs a big spoon one last time into the sweet potatoes before sliding the bowl towards Lopaka.

"Oh, yeah." Lopaka's chair is back down on all fours and he reaches for the bowl in one smooth motion. "And as long as we're in North Kohala," he pauses, shaking the spoon over his plate.

I interrupt, "For King Kamehameha Day?"

"You're not interested in a parade, are you, Meli?" Lopaka reaches over to pinch me.

"This year is special. Teacher said the statue came to North Kohala twenty-five years ago on the King's birthday. Can we go, Aunty Min?" I plead.

"Well, if Uncle promised to help the Sakamotos, of course we all go. But, *aumoe*, Meli, look how late it is, and on a school night. *Ho'omoe*, bed time, sweet dreams."

Why send me off, just when their talk is finally interesting? Who are the Sakamotos? They must be Japanese. I didn't know Uncle had farmer friends in Hawi. Their laughter drifts through the wall. How does Aunty expect me to sleep? I flop around and pin my pillow over my head, which muffles the sounds from the kitchen, but not my excitement. We will celebrate the birthday of the first Hawai'ian king! Every year right before summer break Teacher tells the story of Kamehameha the Great's statue, so I know the words by heart. Her voice rises loud and falls soft at just the right places as her hands tell the story:

"The statue of King Kamehameha the First set sail from Europe to Honolulu in 1880, but the ship was swept up by a storm in the Atlantic Ocean and caught fire. With one arm raised high above its head, the statue went down with the ship in shallow waters near the Falkland Islands. The people of Iolani Palace were planning a big celebration for unveiling the statue on the King's birthday in 1883, so they ordered another. The second statue was delivered to Honolulu right away. After years passed by, local fishermen found the shipwreck and began to salvage what they could. Someone pulled the statue from the sea, scraped off the barnacles, and knew the bronze might bring a good price. Almost thirty years later a British sea captain walking through a scrap yard recognized the figure of the noble man leaning against a wall. He remembered the tale of the fiery shipwreck and the lost cargo. Even though the arm was broken, he bought the statue anyway, hoping to sell it to the Hawai'ian government. But he didn't know another statue from the same mold had already arrived in Honolulu. What do you think the Monarchs in Iolani Palace decided to do with the first statue?"

Teacher always asks this question so all the children can shout back the answer; "They gave the statue to North Kohala to honor his birthplace."

"That's right. The arm was fixed, he was painted, and a pedestal was built at the courthouse in the town of Kapaʻau. Now on King Kamehameha Day people come from all the islands for hula, chanting, and feasts. Crowds line the street from Hawi all the way to Kapaʻau and join the parade. They follow the honored guests who carry their home island's traditional long lei. When they reach the courthouse they drape the statue with their gifts. By the end of the parade, Kamehameha is covered with a rainbow of flowers and leaves."

I can smell the perfumed breeze that blows across the courthouse lawn as I drift off to sleep.

*   *   *

We are bouncing along the road on our way over Kohala Mountain. I am wedged between Līhau, the youngest aunty, and Lopaka. We sit on a stack of mats in the back of Uncle Kō's truck. Blankets rolled between our backs and the cab of the truck form a cozy make-shift couch. Instead of the dripping wet forests of the Hāmākua Coast, this part of the Parker Ranch is on the dry side of the mountain. Cows laze in the shade of scattered trees as we drive through miles and miles of waving grass pasture. Talk story is always good for a long drive, and even though they both know the history of the statue, I start the story anyway.

"You know, there is more your teacher should tell you about Kamehameha the Great, Meli." Lopaka interrupts before I even finish with the sea captain part of the story. "If she leaves out parts, the storyteller misleads you."

"Lopaka, let her be. She's just a *keiki*." Līhau scolds.

"No, she's not. She's grown up enough."

"Okay, but if she has nightmares, I'm gonna be waking you up to sit with her."

"No worries, no scary talk of Moʻokini and Paʻao's hungry gods. Meli's description of the statue reminded me of a man I met at the Honolulu parade last year. I didn't know he was an art professor from the museum. He grabbed me by the elbow and pushed his way through the crowd with me in tow. We stop and stared up at the statue. I'm thinking this guy is a little strange, until he says, 'Ask questions Lopaka. There are layers to every story, especially the ones told from books.' What he said is important, Līhau. Meli needs to understand that the truth is not always the way a story is first told."

"You're right. Continue professor." Līhau wrinkles her nose at Lopaka.

He's so busy talking he misses her teasing.

"He said the problems start at the statue's feet. The King would only wear his sandals when he traveled a long journey on rocky paths, not while he was wearing the sacred feather cape and sash. And the feathers would never touch the ground. Anyway, the statue's sandals aren't even Hawai'ian style."

"Shoes and socks Teacher always says, but that's not the Hawai'ian way either."

"And did you know that the artist who sculpted the statue was studying in Italy?"

"Isn't that where the Romans lived? Why does that matter?" I ask.

"Yes, Romans, not Hawai'ians. So what else is wrong with the statue?" Lopaka asks us.

"Well, I always thought he doesn't look like any *kanaka* I know," Līhau said.

"Of course not. And the artist had a copy of Kamehameha's portrait, and lots of photographs of Polynesians! The professor told me some historians say that the model was half Hawai'ian, but why does the King's statue look like a Roman?"

"That's not *pono*," Līhau says, "especially when the sculptor had the King's picture."

"The face, the nose and cheek bones, they're all wrong. A Hawai'ian king would have a face more like Uncle Kō's," Lopaka finishes with pride in his voice.

"Ha, Lopaka, you are son of Kō. Are you bragging that your face resembles that of a king?" Līhau reaches across and pinches Lopaka. A slap fight between the two erupts, leaving me in the middle ducking their ruckus, all the while thinking about the face of a king.

Now I understand what Lopaka meant about Teacher's story. There was more to know, more to ask, more facts to discover. Her version is only part of the history, part of the truth.

"Look over there," I shout, distracting them from their slapping. "Pueo, eating by the side of the road. He's looking right at us!"

"That's a lucky sign, Meli." Līhau nudges me. "Good news is coming your way."

*   *   *

King Kamehameha Day celebration is always a whirlwind of friends, families, and strangers. Two whole days of dancing, music, and lots of food. We are staying outside of the village of Hawi with the Sakamotos, friends of Uncle Kō. Now that the festival is over, the work begins. Mister Sakamoto and his wife have an avocado orchard. They are *kupuna*, at least Aunty Min's age, and this year the harvest work is too much for them to finish alone. Their grown sons used to work the orchard, but last year they both left for San Francisco.

We pick the pebbled green fruits in the cool morning air. Lopaka and Līhau work all day, but Uncle Kō and Aunty Min spend their afternoons visiting friends. Today they invite me to go for a drive with them after breakfast.

We rumble along the Kohala coast to the sugar company's harbor at Māhukona. As we travel down the road, Aunty Min dips into a bag of *ti* leaves on her lap. She twists and twines a delicate leaf cord as she hums a *mele*. At Māhukona we turn off the main road and continue along a narrow, bumpy track. Uncle Kō slows to a crawl, peering out his side window.

"There they are." Uncle Kō steers the truck to the side of the road. I'm a little confused. Although we are far from any houses, from what Uncle just said and the finished *ti* leaf lei Aunty has woven, I feel as if we are about to greet friends.

"Who are we visiting, Uncle Kō?" I ask following Aunty Min out the passenger door. Across the channel to the west, Haleakalā, the sleeping volcano of Maui, is shrouded in dark clouds.

"We are honoring our ancestors," he says as he leads the way down the trail. "Since the beginning of time our people have sailed thousands of miles across the open ocean. The Polynesian navigators used the signs of nature, the stars in the heavens, the patterns of the ocean, even the birds and fish to guide them here. They erected these rocks in ancient times. This *heiau* is a shrine to mark the way back to their home islands."

Aunty Min is moving slow, picking her way carefully down the rocky trail. Uncle Kō stops so she can catch up to us before he takes off again. "Now, since our people settled," he points in the general direction of the islands that string out beyond Maui, "we have lost our wanderlust and forgotten how to sail by the moon and stars. Years ago, I took Aunty Min to the Marquesas Islands in my boat, but I used a compass, instruments, and charts. I don't know if I could find my way to those islands if all I had were the stars and a sail. And this channel, *'Alenuihāhā*," he points to the ocean between Hawai'i and Maui, "is where the winds and the waters rush between the mountains. The weather here can change fast, and dangerous waves appear from nowhere. I am always watchful in this passage, even though my boat has a powerful engine."

We follow the trail to the ruins of the *heiau*. Stone pillars of different shapes and heights rise tall from a field of rubble, like a group of proud people gazing out to sea. Aunty ties a final knot and lays the *ti* leaf lei on a rock below the closest standing stone with care. We follow Uncle's hand as he points to the horizon.

"These pillars mark the bearings to Tahiti, the Nuku Hiva, Rapa Nui, and other home islands of the Pacific. Remember this place, Meli. The stones honor the courage and skill of the men and women who settled Hawai'i. If you hold this *heiau* in your heart, you will always know how to find your way home."

"Is star navigation what Kele was teaching Miki?" I ask Aunty Min.

"Yes. Kele would be the one to show us how to use these stones, and which stars would guide us across the ocean."

"Do you mean Kele from the Ho'ololi?"

"You know the tale of Pueo too, Uncle Kō?"

"Of course, Meli. Where are you in the story?"

"Pueo found Kolea on the raft and now that he knows which direction to fly he is on his way to find the Ho'ololi."

"Well, tomorrow I will sit with you. I'd like to hear that part again." Uncle Kō sets his hands on my shoulders and points me back up the trail. "Now, time to *hele* on to Hawi."

In the long shadows of late afternoon the Sakamoto's farmhouse is a welcoming sight. After dinner Lopaka picks up a guitar and strums a few chords as an invitation. Līhau joins in with her 'ukulele, and everybody starts singing. My head is full of thoughts of the navigators. I don't want to stay until the last lullaby song, so I slip away to my bed on the screen porch. Hoping for a dream of the ancestors, I curl up to the soft music and fall asleep.

I wake to a chattering in the darkness, followed by a rattle in the leaves of the big tree. An eerie silence follows. Even the crickets outside my window have gone still. My heart races as I wait for the next sound. Was that voice in a dream, or did I awake because someone called my name from high in the breadfruit tree? I am about to sing for Pueo's help, but for some reason I pause and listen. A ree-yow call comes from the edge of the clearing. A lone owl has begun his early morning hunt. One by one the insects start to chirp again, and the thumping in my ears fades away.

From his perch outside my window Pueo has stolen away any chance that I might fall back to sleep. The shadows of night linger under the trees, but out on the lawn, silhouetted against the faint dawn light, I see a figure at the table. I ease the porch door open and tiptoe across the wet grass.

"*Hūi*, Meli."

The light from the kitchen glints off his glasses. "Loloa?"

"You surprised to see me?"

"Yes. I mean no." I sit across from him. "You seem to show up in odd places."

"Don't everybody come to see da parade?"

"I guess, but what are you doing here on the farm?"

"I come to visit Joe, but his pop say he gone to da Mainland. I could ask you da same."

"We're helping with the harvest because Mr. Sakamoto's sons are gone."

"You up early. Singin' with da *ūhini*?"

"No. Pueo's call woke me and he hushed those crickets. Did you hear him?"

"From up in dat big *'ulu* tree, sure did."

"I think he called to me, to make sure I wouldn't forget my dream."

"A good dream?"

"I don't know. I was sitting in a canoe. Pueo was perched in a *hala* tree above me. He wasn't talking words, more like I heard his thoughts. Aunty Min says that's how animals speak to people."

"Most folks don't listen when da animals talk. What did Pueo say, Meli?"

"He said 'Time for the truth. Soon a door will be unlocked and you will meet a beautiful woman. Remember to ask her about your mother.'"

"Sound like dis woman was a friend to your ma. He tellin' you da door is open."

"What door?"

"Truth opens da doors in your life. Like walkin' from one room into da other."

"Or like from inside to outside, a totally different view?"

"Could be like dat."

"Then he said, 'Accept the journey.' Does that mean I have to travel somewhere?"

"How you live da future is a choice you gonna make."

"Well, I must be going on a trip because his last words were, 'Wherever you go, I will always be with you, Meli.' I heard my name just as the owl screeched. Scared me wide awake."

"Where da dream from, Meli?"

"You know, bits and pieces of my day mix in with what the spirits send me. Uncle Kō drove Aunty Min and me to the *heiau* over by Māhukona yesterday. Mostly talk about ocean voyages and navigators from our homeland. Maybe that fed part of my dream, but where did the mysterious woman come from?"

"Don't know 'bout dat, but I do know dis." He slaps his hands on the table. "I gotta go." Loloa leans across the table. "She knows da answer, dat's good." he whispers. "And when da time come, just make a plan." Then he's gone.

I stay at the table and whisper Pueo's message, otherwise the details will fade away and vanish before breakfast. A hint of pale blue sky begins to outline the house. I repeat one sentence, over and over again, "Time for the truth."

The crates are almost full, and we work hard all morning. By lunchtime the harvest is done and the last truck rumbles away. Lopaka drives the Sakamotos and Līhau into town to celebrate. Aunty Min and I clean the kitchen while Uncle Kō reads the newspaper at the table. He likes to read aloud when the news is about Territory politics.

"There's trouble brewing Min. Too many American sailors and pilots, filling up the towns on Oʻahu. Too many bars, too much drinking. Turning life bad for local folk. Listen to this."

I wait while Uncle reads from the article, and interrupt when he shakes out the paper to turn to a new page.

"Where should we sit for the story, Aunty Min? The Sakamotos don't have a *lānai*, and the only comfortable chair is out on the screen porch."

"That will do just fine." she says, drying her hands on a towel. "You and Uncle can sit on the couch. Just don't fall asleep."

"Not a chance." I rush ahead of her to tidy the porch.

"Kō." Aunty Min shakes the top of his paper as she walks past. "Let's not keep Meli waiting." She sets her cup on a metal tray next to the chair. "Remind Uncle where we are in the story, Meli."

I wait for Uncle Kō to settle in. The couch sighs as he sinks into the cushions at the other end. "Kekoa changed back into Pueo with the first sun beams and headed north, but by mid-day he still hasn't found the Ho'ololi. He lands on a scrap of thatch to rest and meets Kolea. She shows Pueo which way to fly."

"I hope Pueo finds that canoe before sunset, Min." Uncle says, crossing his arms and closing his eyes.

Night Visitor

After the excitement of her first day sailing far beyond her home island, Lani was eager for the solitude of her sleeping space. She had so much to learn about living on the Ho'ololi. The crew was like a small village, and with everyone sharing such a small space there had to be rules. Doing her share would not be a problem, but she was used to living on an island where she had lots of room to roam when she wanted to be alone. Being so close to people all the time was new for her. She must remember that unless someone was in danger, or she was asked to join in, she should keep her eyes and ears on her own work. That would be much easier for her father. Unless he was sharing his counsel with Ikaika, Ka'imi liked sitting by himself. Probably best, for although most of the crew believed in him as their spirit guide, not everyone was as comfortable with Ka'imi's habits as Lani. Unlike Ka'imi, Lani tended to be curious. Even now, as she made her way across the *pola* to the stern seat, she found herself eavesdropping.

"You have the star song, Kele. Why were Lani and Ka'imi asked to join this voyage?" Lani's ears perked at the mention of her name. She slowed her steps as she passed behind Miki and Kele.

"Why is that of concern to you, Miki?"

"I don't trust him. I heard Ka'imi conspiring with the captain of the watch this evening, something about a bird. And you know about Lani, she..."

Lani wanted to stay within ear shot. Instead she moved on. Miki's voice gurgled into the sounds of the ocean. Lani adjusted a stiff mat across the opening of the sleeping space and curled into a ball. Perhaps the bird Miki mentioned was the *ʻaumakua* Kaʻimi spoke of yesterday. She would ask her father later. Lani pulled the edge of her *kīhei*, her soft *kapa* shawl, over her head and fell into a deep sleep.

She felt like only a moment had passed when something knocked into her back. Lani was so tired she ignored the disturbance. Another bump against the mat. She woke with a groggy worry that she might have overslept.

"Huh? Time to wake already?" Lani asked, not believing a full watch had passed.

No one answered. Instead of being called to work, another nudge. If the person wasn't Kaʻimi, who had come to the stern seat? This was not the prod of a clumsy foot. The mat shifted as someone reached under and touched her shoulder.

"Lani," the intruder whispered.

"What?"

"It's Kekoa."

"That's a mean joke," Lani hissed. Was this Miki playing a cruel trick on her? Wide awake, her heart raced. "Go away," she commanded the prankster to leave, but his hold on her tightened.

"Please, Lani, hush."

Lani struggled even though the voice sounded like Kekoa's. One hand grabbed her from behind, clamped tight across her mouth before she could cry out, and the other wrenched her arm, shoving her further back under the mat. Lani could barely breathe.

Was Miki right after all? If Kekoa had jumped from a cliff in despair, his spirit could be stuck between the island and the underworld beneath the sea. The hand and the voice must belong to Kekoa's ghost. He had come to haunt her, whisper in her ear while holding her close. The hairs on her neck stood up, the skin on her arms and legs bristled. At first she wrestled in the phantom's clammy grip, but this ghost was strong. If she kept fighting her bones might snap.

Pinned against the hull, she quit struggling. Maybe, if Kekoa's ghost had followed the canoe, he needed help to find his way between this world and the next. As her tense muscles softened, her heart no longer made a rushing noise in her ears. The hand slipped away from her mouth and gathered her long hair away from her face.

"Whisper, Lani, so no one hears you."

"Kekoa?" Her mind whirled as she noticed the warmth of his body.

"How?"

"A spell. I climbed the mountain and asked Kāulamana to bring us together."

"Magic?" Lani still resisted his embrace.

"The night I spent at Kāulamana's is a long story, but right now I'm starving." He hugged her again. "Do you have anything to eat?"

"Oh, it's really you, Kekoa." A ghost wouldn't be hungry. "Give me some room, I've got snacks in one of my bags." She rummaged through the contents until she felt a small gourd that should be stuffed with baked breadfruit in coconut cream. Lani pried at the lid until the gummy sap seal gave way and dipped her finger in. "Try this," she put the gourd in Kekoa's hand and tucked the mat back over them for privacy.

In-between bites Kekoa shared the details of his adventure in a hushed voice. Lani was impressed by Kekoa's courage to climb the mountain and find the magician. Kāulamana had a reputation in the village for love spells with outcomes both good and bad. He described how he accepted a bone-twisting change just to be with her, his first failures at flying, and his first sunset alone on the rocky island. Lani had heard many legends wilder and more fanciful than Kekoa's. Unlike those stories of old, this magic was real and in her arms.

"We're together Lani, just as Kāulamana promised. I can be with you, at least for the nighttime. From now on the journey will be easier. I will never leave you."

While Kekoa whispered his story, slivers of her past pricked Lani at every mention of Kāulamana. In the first memory, she was very little. A woman held her by both hands. As her feet lifted from the ground the world twirled around them, the forest and the sea flashing by, while the woman sang a playful song. The next remembrance was dark and frightening, a rare night full of lightning and crashing thunder. Ka'imi held Lani tight against his chest as he called out that name, over and over again. Shortly after that stormy night Lani and Ka'imi left the island. When they returned, people in the village only whispered the name Kāulamana behind their backs, and with the passage of time Lani forgot the magician was ever part of her life. Anyway, when she was a *keiki*, many mākuahine watched after her. Each of them loved her in a special way, so she held only vague memories of this woman named Kāulamana.

"Lani, are you listening?" Kekoa interrupted her musing. "This is important. You're the only one who can see and hear me at night, to everyone else I'm invisible. The only problem is, I still have a body."

"You mean someone can trip over you? We can't let that happen."

"How will I stay out of the way?"

"No one comes back here. Ka'imi usually sleeps up on the seat instead of down here in the hull, under the mat."

"Does the crew still believe that the spirits join your father?"

"Of course. Tonight he told the captain of the watch about a bird *'aumakua*. From talk I heard, by tomorrow the whole crew will know. If Ka'imi sits with a spirit, they'll stay far away."

"I flew in very low and hopped right down here. I didn't think Ka'imi saw me."

"He spotted you the day we left. An owl joining us during the day is mysterious enough, but no one, not even Ka'imi can know about your change at night. Your human form is a secret between us."

"Then you'll have to remember to whisper. Otherwise the crew will believe you are speaking with the spirits."

Lani secretly wished she had that power. "What about daytime? Can I talk to Pueo?"

"Kāulamana and Kolea understood the sounds I make, but I don't think you will."

"Probably best. Squawking at me would attract attention from the crew. I don't want Miki asking me any questions."

"Why?"

"For some reason we're not the best of friends."

"Oh." Kekoa understood. He had heard Miki's sharp tongue before. "What will I do if the weather turns stormy? Your father might take shelter down here under this mat."

"Tomorrow I'll move the bags and baskets to make a separate space for you. As long as you're quiet he won't mind."

"In the morning I'll stay under the mat until the change. Before I slip out, I'll make sure no one is nearby."

"Can you stay in the air all day?"

"I can, but flying for hours is hard work. I need to eat, but I don't want to bring home birds."

"This morning Ikaika gave me the job of fishing. At the end of the day a few small fish can slip into my basket."

"Fish? That's fine for seabirds Lani, but I need to eat more than that!"

"Don't worry, Kekoa. I can share part of my meals with you. There should be plenty."

"If you ignore me during the day, and we are quiet at night, no one should know I've joined the crew."

Lani and Kekoa held each other tight. Their excitement melted with exhaustion, and they fell into a deep sleep.

Lani awoke to a shaft of sunlight piercing through a gap in the mat. Had Kekoa really been with her, or had she spent the night alone in a vision? She shuffled around, looking for some evidence of Kekoa. Right before she woke up, she had a dream. She remembered sitting in a small canoe, having a conversation with an owl. She started to doubt that his visit was real and became more confused. If Kekoa had come to her last night, she should have dreamed about him, not a bird. Kekoa said she wouldn't be able to talk to Pueo. Her heart ached at the prospect that the visit had been an illusion, or worse yet, that the visitor was a ghost. Fighting back tears, Lani slid the mat aside to face the day. Miki glared down at her from two steps away.

"That cursed bird of your father's just pooped on my head. I'm going to get you for this, Lani."

Doldrums

On the fifth day of the voyage the winds began to falter. By moonrise her sails sagged, and the canoe drifted with the current. The dancing surface of the ocean flattened. The next morning was a dead, windless calm.

"The stars show that the current is moving us to the west," Kele advised Ikaika at their morning meeting.

"What should we do?" Maloka, the captain of the watch, asked.

"We will wait for the wind to find us. Leave the sails raised for shade. Tell the crew to exercise *ahonui*. Be patient and breathe deeply. Once the winds return we will find our way back on course." Ikaika ordered.

Out of the corner of her eye Lani watched Ikaika speaking with Kele, Ka'imi, and the captain of the watch. Every morning and evening they met, sitting together on a mat at the back of the pola, their heads together, discussing the change of the watch. She wondered what decisions were being made.

"I don't understand why we aren't paddling Mākaukau" Lani said as she dropped her lines over the edge. "We are hardly moving. A lazy lure won't attract any fish. Do you think Ikaika will order us to paddle?"

"No, Ho'ololi is too awkward for paddles. Look how far you would reach to dip your blade in the water. The canoe is too heavy to respond. Everyone would eat and drink twice as much for the effort. I am sure Ikaika will tell us to wait until the winds return."

The rest of the day passed without the slightest breeze rippling the water. In the spooky silence the crew on watch lounged under the sails.

The others propped paddles against the rails, draping mats over them to create shade. Without lines to tend or hulls to bail the crew was as still as the sea.

Lani's idle mind craved the texture of a ripe guava. The thought of fruit teased her appetite and a growling stomach answered. On the open ocean, without re-supply at islands, fresh fruit and vegetables disappeared after the first few days. Everything they ate now was dried or salted, served up with the ever-present fish. *Niu* was the only fresh food that kept well at sea. Their fibrous shell repelled the seawater. Once the *niu* was cracked open, the faintly sweet water and brilliant white meat was a real treat. Now the thought of coconut water made Lani's mouth feel drier.

The clouds taunted them. Ever since the canoe had left the village, the squalls had roared by in the distance, pouring their sweet water into the ocean instead of the Hoʻololi. When the cook thumped the giant drinking water gourds, and most of them responded with a hollow sound, Ikaika ordered rationing.

At day's end the change of the watch happened silently without the usual boisterous banter. After dinner with the crew Lani crept back to the stuffy sleeping space with a bowl of *ʻuala*, sweet potato, tucked under her *kīhei* for Kekoa. Because she had dozed off and on all day, she was now wide awake, and anticipated whispering with him into the night. Kekoa had other plans. After flying all day he was famished. Lani squinted in the fading light as he stuffed and chewed until the last morsel disappeared. With a grunt of thanks, he pecked her on the cheek, curled up with his back to her, and was fast asleep, while she sat holding the empty bowl.

With quiet determination the crew began their third day surrounded by the grayness of a fog that blocked the sunrise. Lapaʻau approached Ikaika to ask permission to open the calabash where the *kō*, the sugarcane, was stored.

"I will save plenty of stalks back for planting."

"All of the *kō* is needed for the new island."

"At least let Mākaukau cut two stalks into small pieces, enough for each person," she pleaded.

As Lapaʻau offer a short stick and a blessing to each crew member, Ikaika accepted the wisdom in her request.

"A sweet to soothe both mouth and mind."

Lani gratefully gnawed the sugary stem, for any diversion was appreciated.

The sails had been gathered since there was no need for their shade. Droplets of water collected on Lani's skin. When she licked her lips, all she found was the taste of salt. They floated through the fog. Without even a shadow to show the sun's movement, time crept by. The top of the mast traced subtle patterns in the mist, hypnotizing Lani. She watched the folds of the sail flop back and forth in unison with the mast, a slow dance — reach... dip... pull... lift... reach... dip... pull... lift...

Ka'imi sat with Ikaika and Maloka on a pile of mats stacked against the pola rail. They listened as Kele described the measure of their progress against the stars they had followed the previous night.

"Instead of drifting to the sunset we have begun moving north. A new current works with us, carrying the Ho'ololi back toward the sunrise."

Kele's news of a change in course was encouraging, but Ikaika longed for a wind. He was eager to steer the canoe on a course toward Kai'imi's island, even under the slightest puff of wind. The morning air hung perfectly still, heavy with the mist. By mid-day, without relief from the steamy heat, his crew would sag as limp as the sails. Drifting added days to the voyage. The heat was taking a toll. Even with *ahonui*, their provisions would soon reach the half-way mark.

While Ikaika discussed the rationing of food and water with Maloka, Ka'imi's gaze wandered past his friend to where Pueo had landed on the *manu*. The owl cautiously side-stepped his way down to the edge of the stern seat. Unsettled by Pueo's early return, and sensing a presence in the swirling mist behind them, Ka'imi excused himself. He worked his way across the canoe and settled next to Pueo on the back edge of the seat. For the longest time they stared out into the gray. Ka'imi had no doubt Pueo was *'aumakua*, an ancestor spirit sent to protect Lani. He had tried to talk with Pueo before in the usual way. He often stepped over to the realm of the spirits for guidance and was familiar with the path to reach them. Ka'imi could will the physical world to slip away. He would close his eyes, and with a shiver or a shudder, sometimes with a thump like being too close to lightning, the spirit world surrounded him. Then, with eyes wide open, he could speak freely with whoever was present. Ka'imi was unfamiliar with reluctant spirits. He wondered why

Pueo was never waiting on the other side when he stepped through. He glared at the bird.

"Do you need to tell me something?" Ka'imi spoke aloud.

Swiveling his head in a most unsettling manner, Pueo uttered a series of clicks and barely audible squawks.

"Canoe followed," were the words that Ka'imi heard.

"What?" Shocked to hear Pueo's answer, Ka'imi looked around. The nearest crew members on this side of the canoe were staring. Everyone except Lani quickly looked away. Ka'imi knew their response only too well. Sometimes he talked to himself, but usually he was speaking with someone on the other side. Even though Ikaika believed in him as their spirit guide, some of the crew found his invisible friends unsettling. Ka'imi was the only one to hear the owl's words, but Lani still looked his way, her expression suggesting that she expected more.

"What is following us? Ikaika will want to know."

"War canoe." Keeping his eyes on Ka'imi, Pueo shifted his feet to untwist his neck before he continued. "Noticed yesterday on long flight. Much closer now."

"Do you know what island they call home?"

"Maybe atolls to the sunset. Strong warriors in fast canoe, here soon."

"What do they want?" Ka'imi asked, hesitation tinged his voice.

"Who knows." A moment passed before Pueo added, "No good."

Ikaika watched Ka'imi pick his way back across the *pola* to the pile of mats where he sat with Maloka and Kele. Routine becomes second nature on a sailing vessel. Pueo's early return and Ka'imi's obvious conversation with the bird marked a noticeable change in an otherwise drab start to the day. Ka'imi's furrowed brow conveyed a new worry. Ikaika braced for trouble as Ka'imi sat down and spoke without any of the usual pleasantries.

"Pueo spotted a war canoe sailing from the atolls to the west. He believes they will be upon us before nightfall."

All of the crew believed in magic, but not all trusted in a benevolent outcome. The ominous threat of visitors brought the mutterings of the crew out into the open. Maloka was the first to challenge Ka'imi. "How do we know the bird has not led the warrior canoe to us? Not everyone on the crew accepts him as a valuable scout."

"This is true. One of my students says this bird has brought bad luck to the voyage." Kele added.

"Pueo's words give us an advantage, otherwise why would he bother to warn Ka'imi?" Ikaika spoke in support of Pueo. The days spent in the doldrums had weakened the spirit of his crew, causing doubt and confusion. Ka'imi's talk with the owl followed by this hushed discussion could create a division between those who trusted and those who might challenge the loyalty of the *'aumakua*. If the war canoe attacked, the crew of the Ho'ololi must work together without hesitation.

Ikaika moved to the center of the *pola* and spoke loudly so all would hear.

"Gather around," Ikaika waited as all the crew came closer. His squared shoulders and broad chest asserted absolute authority. "I believe Pueo serves Ho'ololi as a guide." He searched each face, and held the gaze of the few crew members that scowled back defiantly until he was sure everyone agreed. Miki was the only one who hung her head, refusing to meet his eyes or assent with a nod. Lani continued to stare at Ikaika, but in her expression Ikaika saw confidence as if she knew more about the owl's purpose than Ka'imi. Puzzled by her response, Ikaika nodded to Lani before he returned to his place on the mats and the problem at hand.

"We are in agreement. The war canoe is where the danger lurks," Ikaika spoke first, inviting advice from the three who sat with him.

"Surely they have no need for food or water. I know the location of the atolls," Kele said. "They're too close to home to be lacking provisions."

"Then what do these warriors want? A thirst for blood? Do they dare tempt us?" Maloka thumped the mat in front of him with both fists, the veins on his muscled arms pulsed.

"Consider our crew. Can we risk a fight?" Ka'imi asked, hoping for a more peaceful solution.

"Worse yet, I have heard of raids where only the strongest men are seized." Maloka sniffed hard through his nose, his upper lip curled in a menacing sneer before he continued. "Our *mana*, our spirit energy, is known to be great. If we were taken for sacrifice, our bones would be a gift to the gods!"

"We cannot afford to lose our strongest men to either battle or capture." Ikaika's voice remained calm. "Who would control the steering paddles and sails if the weather turns stormy?"

"What if we offer them *pua'a*, the black sow and her piglets, stowed away at the bow?" Ka'imi suggested in a quiet voice.

They all stared at Ka'imi in surprise. His suggestion might work.

"A bribe to leave us in peace?" Ikaika asked.

A black pig was coveted, more valuable than other colors, and half of her piglets were black. This black sow would deliver generations of black pigs. And that was just her ceremonial value. *Pua'a* flesh was also food.

"Temporary camps survive with fish and fowl, but a flourishing village needs pigs. They should see the value of our gift if we offer them the *pua'a*. If they accept the pigs instead of a fight, we would keep our full crew. But, no *pua'a* means no village," Ikaika reminded them.

"When we raise the island some of us could settle," Maloka suggested.

Following the path of Ikaika's strategy Kele proposed, "If I had a small crew of the strongest men, I could sail the Ho'ololi back home. In time we would return with more pigs and more people."

"Yes, Kele, you could guide them back," Ikaika agreed. "And the new island gardens could be planted with the slips and cuttings, the seeds, and tubers. We could fish and gather food from the sea until you returned."

Only three of the four agreed aloud. Ka'imi managed a tight-lipped nod. A vision had shimmered in the early morning fog before he spoke to Pueo, and the images shone again before him now. The island rose from the sea just as before, except this time they failed to make landfall. For some reason the Ho'ololi turned away and they sailed home, their goal of settling the new island unfulfilled. What they had just agreed to, splitting the crew and leaving a small group behind on the island, opposed this vision. Ka'imi couldn't speak for or against the new plan. Ikaika searched his friend's face before ending the discussion with orders.

"We cannot outrun this war canoe, and we must keep our strongest men. The pigs we can do without. These strangers are to be treated as guests. Welcome and feed them, but don't be foolish. Remain watchful to their real intent. Enough talk. Alert the crew and prepare."

As the day progressed, all eyes searched as the fog gradually burned off to a dull white haze. The warrior vessel first showed on the horizon as a dark dot. With the passing hours the dot grew in size. Soon everyone could see that the canoe was a long single hull with a single outrigger. Paddlers pulled on both sides in unison. The strangers would soon be alongside.

Ikaika called for his crew to shake out the sails. Without a wind the raised sails were only for show; like a peacock fanning his tail feathers. With her sails unfurled the Hoʻololi was impressive, even though she sat like a tern on a glassy sea.

A puff of wind caressed the canoe, ruffling Pueo's sensitive feathers. Nobody else noticed that the calm of the doldrums was about to end. The Hoʻololiʻs crew stared in amazement as the war canoe glided silently alongside. The exotic crew shouted "Kariki Ua." They raised their paddles and stood in unison, all of them women.

Tricked

Ka'imi had heard of women who shunned their traditional roles of lovers and mothers, choosing instead a mercenary life of raiding and trading. Recalling the fate of the men who encountered the warriors in those stories weakened his knees. He slumped back on the stern bench.

"Now what?" Ka'imi asked no one in particular and gestured to Lani to come sit with him. Ikaika and Maloka's plan had been based on their combat experience with male warriors. These fierce-looking women had momentarily stunned the Ho'ololi crew with the element of surprise.

Five of the warriors swung their paddles over their heads. The butt of each shaft bristled with a menacing carved figure, a big carved gri macing face that also served as a hook. In one smooth arcing motion they reached across to the Ho'ololi, grappled the side board and pulled, coupling the canoes together. Without waves or wind to challenge the connection, the two canoes became one.

From where Lani sat, she could barely see the warriors as they prepared to board the Ho'ololi. Curious, she stood up on the bench, steadying herself on Ka'imi's shoulders. One woman stood out from all the rest. She was tall, and her wild hair stuck out from her head as if a gale wind blew. Ropes of tiny shells hung from her neck, forming a shield over her chest. Blueish-black geometric tattoos and reddish-purple scars covered her body from head to toe. Lani couldn't tell where her patterned loin cloth and cape began or ended. When this most decorated warrior shouted unintelligible words, "Tia rai raeka," two women jumped forward. For a moment the wild looking woman's gaze fell upon Lani. Struck by Wild-One's fierce glare, Lani crouched behind Ka'imi's shoulder, regretting that her curiosity had caught the warrior leader's attention.

"Katootoonga," Wild-One barked at the two warriors as she jumped across to the Ho'ololi. They followed, and the three strode across the pola to stand in front of Ikaika and Maloka.

Lani peered around Ka'imi again. Wild-One muttered to the shorter of the two women. The Short-One stepped forward and addressed the captain.

"What island have you sailed from?" Short-One interpreted her leader's question.

Not only did Short-One look like the people from Lani's island, but Lani understood her. Short-One spoke their language. Lani kept her eyes on Ikaika as he considered the visitor's question. He was taller than anyone else in her village. She was impressed by his courage. Unarmed, and a full head shorter than the warrior leader and her guard, he remained fearless. These were the fiercest strangers Lani had encountered. Her heart beat in her stomach.

"We come from the south, the isles of Hiva. And you, where are your islands?"

Short-One spoke softly to the other two. Wild-One directed two sentences to Short-One, while holding the captain's eyes.

Her interpreter faced Ikaika and without answering his question asked bluntly, "Where are you sailing? For what purpose?"

The good manners of sharing small talk before asking a direct question were being overlooked. Ikaika felt the Ho'ololi's voyage should be of no concern to the warriors. He ignored their rudeness as well as her questions.

"Come sit, share drink with me in the shade of the sail," Ikaika gestured to the far side of the *pola*. "We will visit and later we will share a meal."

Short-One turned her back on Ikaika and translated. A snarling leer flashed across Wild-One's dark face, and then changed into a broad smile, revealing four gleaming white canines, each of them filed to a point. Lani gulped. A smile was supposed to be friendly. Wild-One nodded to Ikaika and the group moved out of Lani's sight.

The Wild-One's stare left a mark on Lani like a hot coal that jumps from a fire. The way the warrior's charcoal-black eyes had snagged her reminded Lani of that brief moment before a hook digs itself into soft flesh. She tried to stay out of sight, but hiding during her watch was impossible. She couldn't shake the feeling that Wild-One was reeling her in like a helpless fish. Every time she looked toward Wild-One, those glittering black eyes pierced her. To avoid being skewered, Lani tried to keep her head down and stay as far away as she could.

Soon after the leaders had moved to the shade of the sail, another two warriors came aboard and fixed a line to the Hoʻololi. As the women on the outrigger paddled, the line grew taut. Like clasped hands, the warriors towed the Hoʻololi and the canoes moved toward the west as one. Warriors guarded the rail where the line was tied to the Hoʻololi. They stood with their paddles held like staffs in front of them, the blades on the deck and the menacing carved ends high above their heads.

As scared as she was of Wild-One, Lani was also fascinated by the warrior's strange language and bizarre body markings. The words exchanged between Ikaika and Wild-One seemed peaceful enough, without any shouts or threats. Short-One sat between them, interpreting. The warrior guard stood behind Wild-One, and Maloka and Kele sat behind Ikaika. Once drinks were brought, the talk was over. Wild-One dismissed Short-One and reclined in the shade. The Hoʻololi crew went about what appeared to be their usual duties, but Lani could see that they were preparing for the night as Ikaika had ordered.

All this time, while Ikaika entertained the warrior leader, Lani worked side-by-side with the cook. With a sharpened shell they chopped dried fish on a hardwood platter and swept the pieces into a big bowl. The only noise shared between them was the clacking of their tools. Mākaukau had asked her to help with the evening meal. Twice as many people would hold out their bowls tonight, and hospitality required that plenty of food be served. From where she stood Lani could see Pueo. He perched on the *manu* near Kaʻimi, both of them as far away from the warriors as possible. Pueo sat with Kaʻimi until Ikaika excused himself from his guests and went back to sit with Kaʻimi on the stern. As Ikaika approached, Pueo flew off and rose high above the canoes, unnoticed by the visitors. Lani wondered what Pueo knew about the warriors' intent.

Lani glanced at the warriors' canoe. Miki was sitting with Short-One in the bow of the outrigger, their heads close together. Lani couldn't hear their conversation, though something felt wrong. Miki leaned in and cocked her head, giving Short-One her full attention.

"I know it's none of my business," Lani said, interrupting the clack-clack-clack of shell against wood, "but I wish I could hear what's going on between those two." Lani pointed with her chin toward the warrior canoe. Mākaukau straightened to follow her gaze.

"'*Eā*, that girl Miki make me wonder sometime." Mākaukau returned to his chopping.

"No good is going to come from that talk," Lani said as she reached into the gourd for another dried fish.

*   *   *

There was a reason Miki had been lured over to the warrior canoe. Before dismissing Short-One from the group at the sail, Wild-One had pulled her back and hissed instructions in her ear. She was to invite a certain Ho'ololi woman back to their outrigger. Short-One must convince this woman to join them. Only then could Wild-One's plan proceed. Short-One cast her eyes about the Ho'ololi crew. Ah, there she was, the only person who looked eager to come forward and meet the strangers. Short-One had gestured, and Miki was thrilled to be invited over to the warrior's canoe.

"Wait, slow down! What do you mean, she wants the women?" Miki asked again, sure that she had misunderstood what Short-One said.

That morning, when Ikaika had gathered the crew to share Pueo's warning of the approaching canoe, he had put them to work at tasks that needed to be completed before nightfall in order to best defend the crew. The Ho'ololi leaders were sure the men were the target of the warriors. As they went about their regular duties subtle changes were to be made. Because Miki and Lapa'au shared a sleeping place in one of the hulls, they were directed to move their sleeping gear onto the *pola*. Except for Ka'imi and Lani's space under the stern seat, most of the other sleeping places had been rearranged. The strongest men had moved their gear. Until the warriors left, they would sleep forward in the hulls where they could best protect themselves and the cargo.

Short-One's rapid words revealed the Wild-One's intent. In disbelief, Miki interrupted again, "So your leader wants the three of us?"

"Of course. Haven't you been listening? We only add women to our crew. Anyway, you don't want to stay with those men. Miki, don't be a fool. You weren't picked to help navigate, you were chosen because your crew is going to settle a new island. You'll be working the land and raising babies for the rest of your life when you could be exploring the ocean. The only thing you'll need the stars for is wishing that you had sailed with us."

Miki regretted that she had been so quick to share her passion for wayfinding with Short-One. In the excitement of preparing for the voyage she had never questioned why, out of all the other students, she had been chosen to join the crew. Even then she had been too busy boasting. Short-One's harsh words made the reason she was included clear. But she wasn't ready to settle down, have babies, and watch after *keiki*. A life somebody else had planned for her would start once they landed on Ka'imi's island. Perhaps if she became a warrior she would have another choice.

"You'll be no better off than those pigs." Short-One gestured towards the bow of the Ho'ololi. "Is that what you want?"

"No." Indignant at the comparison, Miki decided to side with Short-One and what in her mind would be the winning canoe.

Wild-One had picked the proudest of the three women, a strategy that had worked. By luring Miki into joining them, the warrior's plan was set in motion. Like a fish that bites the hook because of a shiny flash, Miki had taken their bait. Short-One began to conspire with Miki on the next step, how to approach and persuade Lapa'au to go along with the idea.

⁂

Ka'imi reclined on the stern seat with Ikaika. From where he sat the women on the outrigger were hidden by the sail. He didn't need to see Miki's actions to sense a shift in the energy surrounding the vessels. Other than the obvious threat from the presence of the warriors, no vision came to explain an ominous weight pressing on his chest. Ka'imi held Ikaika's arm as he rose to leave.

"I cannot join you at dinner. I urge you to be cautious," Ka'imi's eyes darted. He bit his lip as he continued. "Before you eat with our guests tonight I must warn you," Ka'imi paused. He was frustrated that he had no details to offer Ikaika. "You spoke earlier of a threat. There is another danger you have not planned for."

"Your visions serve me well old friend." Ikaika took Ka'imi's hand from his arm. "I will be cautious, but remember, these warriors are just women."

Ka'imi feared that Ikaika had misjudged the women. Although he often slept on the stern seat when seas were calm, tonight the plank felt exposed. After watching the last glow of the twilight he decided to sleep in the hull. Ka'imi jumped down and as he reached for the mat he heard a rustle.

Warned by the thump of Ka'imi's feet, Kekoa scrambled into his space on the other side of the stacked mats and bags. Unable to relax with Ka'imi so close, he twitched with nervous energy.

"Don't add to my irritation, Spirit, be still." Ka'imi spoke to what he believed to be the *'aumakua.*

"What bothers you?" Kekoa asked.

There was a familiar tone to the voice. During the day Ka'imi understood the clicks and calls of the owl and was not surprised for he believed Pueo to be Lani's *'aumakua.* Now he wondered if the bird took another form at night. "I hear you rustle about. I am in no mood for any mysteries tonight." Ka'imi waited, hoping the owl would speak again.

The curious behavior of the *'aumakua* added to Ka'imi's anxiety over the presence of the warriors, as well as his premonition of violence. He was restless until he heard Lani slide the mat back. Relieved she had decided to avoid the visitors after dinner, Ka'imi moved over to make room. With Lani safe under the mat he fell into a deep sleep.

A vivid image of a woman almost awakened Ka'imi. He struggled to stay on the dream side, longing for the woman to come closer. He focused on her radiant beauty, captivated as she approached. *Oho,* he called out, the woman was his wife! Many years had passed since they were together, but he could never forget her charms. Ka'imi clung to the moment, gazed upon her silken skin, and searched her dark eyes with his. Her full lips formed a silent word, and then he clearly heard his name, "Ka'imi." Flattered that his wife still called his name, he smiled and reached out. Trying to hold on to both the woman and the dream, Ka'imi felt her hand slip through his. He woke to mayhem.

Kidnapped

Everything happened so fast. One minute Lani was asleep beside Ka'imi and the next, she was roughly pulled by her feet from their sleeping space. Instinctively, she had called out her father's name. As one hand found the loop on her bag, the other grasped for Ka'imi, but she lost her grip on his hand. Clutching her bag with both hands, Lani hoped the cordage would snag on something and anchor her to the canoe. A coarse sack pulled over her head, smothering her last cry for help. Tossed up like a sack of *taro*, she bounced painfully on what must be a warrior's shoulder. Each running stride crushed her ribs. She held fast to her bag. Screeched battle cries and the sickening thud of wood on flesh gave Lani some hope she would be saved. Then her captor landed with a jarring stop. Without care or caution she was dumped in the bottom of a hull. The unintelligible language of the warriors surrounded her. Shouts of her own crew grew distant. Lani could barely breathe. A strong moldy smell from the coarse cloth over her face made her gag. She heard the cadenced splash of paddles. Lying in a slimy puddle of water, Lani hugged her gear bag and shivered with fright. She had been kidnapped.

*   *   *

Aboard the Ho'ololi the crew called out to each other. When the warriors had rushed across the *pola* with Lani, they had bashed two of the crew aside with the wicked blunt ends of their paddles. Still crumpled where they fell, those men were stunned and bleeding. No one was sure what had happened. A rising wind added to their confusion.

Ka'imi ran forward shouting, "Lani is taken."

The captain of the watch yelled, "Miki and Lapa'au, too."

"Quiet." Ikaika roared. In the silence that followed the distinct sound of paddles pricked their ears.

Ikaika regretted their behavior at dinner. He had decided to entertain the warriors. The men had allowed themselves to be fooled into trusting them. Charmed by Wild-One and her guard's flattery, they were lulled into believing the only loss they would suffer by morning would be the pigs. None of the crew knew of Miki's treason.

Miki had convinced Lapa'au that joining the warriors was Lani's idea. She described in great detail what would happen if Lapa'au decided to stay behind. Miki's words made Lapa'au unwilling to become the lone woman on the Ho'ololi.

Anticipating Ikaika's orders, the crew sprang to the sails before he finished shouting commands. Kele gazed skyward and fixed their location in his mind for the day they would resume their journey north. A gust of wind caught the sails, as if the gods supported the chase, and the canoe responded. One hull of the vessel lifted as the Ho'ololi pivoted toward the west. As nimble as she felt to the crew, their canoe was heavy and slow compared to the outrigger. But if the winds held, their sails would not tire while the outrigger's paddlers would. With luck they would catch sight of the warriors late tomorrow. The future of the new village depended on retrieving their women.

*   *   *

Ka'imi's chest felt hollow. Had the goddess abandoned them? This morning's vision served no purpose. Nothing had warned him of the arrival of the warriors or their intent. And why did he dream of his wife and reach for her instead of waking to grasp his daughter's hand? Without any answers he crawled back to the stern.

Kekoa had stayed crammed in his hiding place behind the stack of mats. He heard the crew shouting, but their words were muffled. Who was returning to the sleeping space, Lani or Ka'imi? He risked discovery and whispered, "What happened?"

"Warriors have taken Lani," Ka'imi groaned. "All the women are gone."

"I've lost her again." Kekoa's voice sank with sadness.

"Is this voyage cursed? First we lost the winds, now the women. Is your strength, *'aumakua*, fading as well?" Ka'imi had never doubted the power of the gods or the spirits and the silence of the *'aumakua* only added to his misery.

"Ka'imi," Kekoa blurted, "I'm not a powerful spirit. I'm just the boy you know from the village."

Ka'imi listened as Kekoa told the story of his love and the despair that drove him to seek Kāulamana's magic. As the words spilled from Kekoa's *mo'olelo*, Ka'imi regretted his selfish actions. Ka'imi had not considered Kekoa and his love for Lani when he encouraged the *ali'i*, the village leaders, to choose her to join the Ho'ololi crew. He had only considered the dangers she might face if he left her behind. Their home island was unsafe, and the rule of the *ali'i* was unstable. Fine men, like Ikaika, sailed on the crew. Once they settled the new island, Lani and her family would be close to him as he grew old. When he chose the voyage for Lani, it was his own future he sought to secure.

Ka'imi recalled Lani's sadness the first night they sailed. When Ikaika gave Lani the duty of fishing, another decision he had encouraged, a new dedication had filled her face. He had hoped Lani would appreciate Ikaika's goodwill for her future. Acceptance isn't the same thing as joy. Lani's laughter had only returned when Pueo arrived. Now he understood the change he had seen. Lani held no special feelings for any other man. Kāulamana's choice of spells, the daily change from boy to owl and back again, was the best way for them to be together, right under everyone's nose!

"I've been such a fool." Ka'imi squinted in the dim starlight, but could not see the boy.

"So have I," Kekoa replied.

As he listened to Kekoa's voice, Ka'imi wondered how Kāulamana's magic worked.

"Do you have form, does a body come across with you at night?" Ka'imi reached out in the general direction of Kekoa's voice.

"Oh yes," Kekoa said, grasping Ka'imi's hand, "and staying out of your way has been difficult."

Ka'imi pulled his hand away from Kekoa's touch and listened while he continued.

"With your help Ka'imi, we can rescue Lani and the others."

"Their outrigger will be far beyond the horizon by sunrise," Ka'imi said.

"I can easily fly that far and find the warriors. When I return, you must convince Ikaika to follow me. I will fly back and forth all day to guide the Ho'ololi to the women."

"You are our only chance."

Ka'imi remembered standing on the stone platform when the *ali'i* had selected the three women for the new settlement. Lapa'au was a compassionate healer. As the oldest woman, she would become an ideal matriarch. Miki had many skills on the ocean as a paddler and navigator. Children who carried her clever and aggressive nature would be hard workers and strong warriors. Lani was kind and agreeable. She had inherited Ka'imi's skill for fishing at an early age. If she failed to develop his powers of vision, perhaps her children would carry on the gift. So each woman was unique, possessing her own special traits that would be passed forward for generations. And the same was true for the men on the crew. The *ali'i* were sure that as time passed, by the birth of the third or fourth child, the new village would begin to flourish with diversity. Even though the future of the new island's lineage could be changed by Kāulamana's magic, none of that mattered if Pueo failed to find the women.

The Chase

In the first light before sunrise, Kekoa pulled the mat tight before rummaging through Lani's food gourds. He heard the morning crew as they assembled on the *pola*. Last night they had abandoned the stars that led north to Ka'imi's island. Kele's voice rose above the others.

"With the mast toward that bright dawn star, the swell will come from there. The sun will rise at our backs as we sail toward the warrior canoe and rescue our women."

Only one of Lani's lumpy bags remained in the sleeping space. In search of breakfast Kekoa quietly fingered through the contents: shell knives, a bundle of bone awls, wooden bowls, and finally what he was looking for, a sealed gourd. Using the sharp edge of a thick shell, he pried at the sap that glued the lid and popped it open. Stirring the sticky contents with his finger, he sniffed. Whatever she had packed away hadn't molded. He pinched out a small amount. Bits of dried banana, mango, and papaya softened on his tongue. Shaking the fruit into his mouth, he emptied the gourd in a couple of chomps. Lucky for him he ate fast, for just as he pressed the lid back on the sticky rim, his fingers changed into flight feathers, the gourd falling with a soft thud. He peeked around the edge of the mat to be sure everyone was still on the pola. Pueo hopped up to the stern seat. Spreading his wings, he caught the wind and wheeled away from the canoe. The chase had begun.

* * *

The first rays of the sun had fanned out across the clouds on the horizon. A brisk wind blew with white-capped waves speckling the dark blue water. The Ho'ololi skimmed along with the familiar whoosh of waves along the hulls and the crew braced against the spray off the bow. Ikaika waited as Ka'imi came forward to stand behind the rest of the crew where they gathered around him on the *pola*.

"Ka'imi has spoken with the *'aumakua*." Ikaika pointed toward the disappearing bird. He gestured for the men to clear a path so Ka'imi could join him. "We must find Lani, Lapa'au, and Miki. Can the *'aumakua* help us?" Ikaika asked.

"I have taken his counsel. Pueo will guide us to the warrior canoe."

Ikaika nodded, his thoughts a tangle of life or death decisions that would unravel as the day unfolded. First, he had to trust the owl to lead them to the war canoe. Not only Ka'imi's daughter was at risk, though her face came first to his mind. To win back their women could mean a bloody battle, especially against those brazen warriors. The fight could go either way. The gods choose, but the Ho'ololi crew was ready to sacrifice themselves. Even with victory the effort would use up precious food and fresh water. Days might pass before they returned to their course leading to the island. Rains must come soon if they were to re-fill the water gourds. A final question tugged at Ikaika's heart. Would Lani survive to continue the journey?

*   *   *

Pueo zigged and zagged in a westerly direction until he spotted his quarry, a few hours after leaving the Ho'ololi. He flew in tight circles. No human below would notice a solitary bird high in the sky, but Pueo could see every detail. A lump of mats or sacking lay between empty seats near the middle of the canoe. A handful of women were idle while the rest propelled the canoe forward with strong even strokes. The Wild-One stood at the stern. He had found the warriors' canoe, but they were a great distance from where he had expected. Their course angled the span of two hands from the windward path the Ho'ololi had sped along all night. With every wasted moment the distance between the canoes widened. He must return as fast as he could.

Ka'imi was waiting on the stern seat. "Warriors tricked Ikaika." Pueo said as soon as he landed on the manu. "Outrigger cuts across swells. Must change course," Pueo instructed Ka'imi, then he tucked his head and rested as Ka'imi went forward to relay his message.

"Last night when we followed the sound of the warrior's paddles we traveled the wrong way," Ka'imi explained to Ikaika. "With the wind at our back we were sure of an easy chase. During the night they turned."

Ikaika spoke to the crew. "Pueo has found the warrior's canoe. Maloka, change course to follow him. We will fight them before nightfall."

"Leave when you are ready," Pueo opened his eyes as Ka'imi spoke to him from the hull below, "but hurry. This day is slipping away."

Pueo ruffled his feathers and lifted off without a word. The next flight was shorter. He approached the outrigger from high above. The warriors still paddled at a furious pace. This time he decided to risk seeking out Lani, to give her a sign that help was on the way. With the sun at its zenith, Pueo began to spiral down. If anyone on the canoe looked up, he hoped to be hidden in the sun's glare. As he wheeled closer, the splash and shine from the paddles slowed. For some reason the warriors had stopped paddling. The shrill sound of an argument erupted.

*   *   *

The sun beat straight down. A warrior pulled the wet sack from Lani's head, cut the cord binding her wrists, and lifted her from the floor of the canoe. She wobbled on unsteady knees, bracing against women seated on each side. Gulping in fresh air, she squinted. The bright sunlight hurt her eyes.

Lani heard the sound of a familiar laugh. She shifted her feet to look toward the bow. Miki sat just a couple yards away, taking a long swig from a drinking gourd. While she looked at Lani, Miki leaned over to share a private joke with Short-One. Lani heard confidence in Miki's laugh, and her own situation was clear. Miki had chosen to join the warriors, conspired in Lani's kidnapping, and betrayed the Ho'ololi.

Miki took another long drink and wiped the liquid from her lips with the back of her hand. She reached across, poked Short-One, and they both roared with laughter. The warrior sitting behind Miki stopped paddling to join in. Infuriated, Lani charged forward. After only a couple of steps she was yanked back, her fists flailing just short of Miki's face. A warrior held Lani firmly by a hank of hair, allowing her to lunge forward, then reeling her back. Because Lani's furious struggles amused the warriors, Wild-One allowed a break from paddling.

Like a bold beaked bird, Short-One jumped up, her hand snaked out, and in a flash she tore Lani's kolea pendant from her neck. Landing back on her seat, she tied a knot in the broken cord. The warriors cheered as she slipped the necklace over her own head.

Goaded on by Short-One, Miki set her drinking gourd on her seat and stood just out of Lani's reach. Lapa'au sat a few rows behind Miki, her eyes down. She wanted no part of this fight.

"How could you do this, Miki?" Lani's anger rose, fueled by the loss of Kekoa's gift. "How could you betray your own people?"

"The only reason we were chosen for the voyage was to have babies on the new island. That might be fine for you, Lani. Not for me, not right now. I'm *ho'okele*; I should be sailing the ocean."

"Hah! Miki, you're the student, not the navigator. We were chosen to settle an island given to our people by a goddess."

"Raising *pua'a* and *keiki* might be your choice Lani. That kind of life bores me."

While they squabbled, a warrior had squatted down behind Lani. She started to pull items from Lani's bag, examining them and handing them out. Miki's eyes darted. She gawked as Lani's tools flew through a dozen hands. Lani followed Miki's gaze.

"Hey, leave my stuff alone!" she cried out.

A couple of warriors taunted Lani as they tossed her favorite bone hammer back and forth over her head.

"Too short, can't paddle a canoe."

"Too little to pound poi."

"Waa-waa, cry-baby, tell your *makuahine*, ha-ha-ha."

Breaking free from her captor's hold, Lani lunged toward the woman pilfering her bag. The warrior grinned at her. The tattooed welts on her chin stretched as she pulled a bundle from the bag. Lani's heart skipped a beat. The next few seconds as the warrior raised the *ko'i* for all to see passed in slow motion.

The warrior stood, swinging the stone tool up with a menacing sneer, and Lani stumbled to a halt within the towering woman's reach. The *ko'i* fell in a deadly arc aimed at Lani's skull. She jumped sideways to escape the blow, one foot finding an empty seat, the other on the hull's edge. A screech and a blur of feathers flew between them. The *ko'i* tumbled, landing on the floor of the hull with a thud. Shocked, the warrior cried out as blood spurted from the red gashes raked across her face. Pueo's talons had found their target. Before anyone could stop her, Lani dove off the canoe, swimming for her life. She knew her escape would be short-lived, but she was ready for a fight.

Confused by the attack, the woman held her face, blood dripping from her elbows. The two taunting warriors rushed to jump in after Lani.

"Stop!" Wild-One shouted as she grabbed the warrior's arm. "Let her go. The ocean can have her."

Denied the sport of pursuing Lani, the warriors returned to their seats. The women who had seized her goods during the fracas stashed them away before picking up their paddles.

Miki sat on an empty seat. The seat across from her remained empty and she looked to Short-One for a cue. "Is there an extra paddle?"

Short-One shrugged, following Lapa'au to tend to the bloody woman. She was thinking of how quick Wild-One had handed Lani over to the ocean. Just yesterday the young girl had been an object of desire. Now she was fish food. No, she would not sit by Miki. Better to help the medicine woman and show her allegiance to the warriors. Short-One's duty to these warriors was to serve as a translator. What if Lapa'au proved herself to be more valuable? Short-One might be seen as an extra mouth to feed. She had been around Wild-One long enough to know how her whims varied from day-to-day. She would distance herself from Miki until Wild-One decided how the new one, the girl with no *mālama*, no loyalty, fit into their group. Short-One fingered the shell pendant that hung from her neck. She did not want to feed the fish.

Hilo Holiday

"Well, Meli, why the big eyes?" Aunty Min asks.

I had ducked into the pillows when Aunty Min's face grew fierce, and her fist followed an arc as the adze swung through the air. "I think the *kūpuna* made a terrible mistake when they picked Miki to go on the voyage." I straighten up before I continue. "I don't care if she was clever. She betrayed her crew!" I hadn't liked that Miki girl from the beginning. Neither did Lani, and now I know why.

"Miki didn't do right, did she?" Uncle Kō asks. "She believed the poison tongue of Short-One."

"Why did Lani pick a fight? Wouldn't keeping quiet in Wild-One's canoe be safer than jumping into the ocean?"

"Lani had no friends on that outrigger, Meli. There was no safe choice." Uncle Kō stretches his legs and pushes himself up off the couch. "What do you think, Min?"

"You choose to be *pono*, especially when what might be safe don't feel right," Aunty Min gathers her tea cup and scoots to the edge of her chair. "Lani decided to take her chances in the water."

"Lopaka's back from town," Uncle Kō says as a pick-up truck rumbles into the driveway. "I sure hope he stopped by that market. Enough vegetables and broth. I'm hungry for *poi* and *kalua pua'a*."

"Shush, Kō, a few more vegetables aren't going to hurt anyone." Aunty Min gives him a playful slap on the belly, "especially you."

Being a guest at the Sakamoto's farm is a new experience for me. They were born here, but their parents are from Japan. Instead of *poi* and sweet potato they eat rice, and lots of vegetables, sometimes with thin glassy noodles, sometimes with fat chewy noodles. Before we came to visit, Aunty Min had reminded me to be polite.

"If the food you are served at the farm tastes different from what we eat at home, remember your manners, Meli. Accept what is on your plate. With a smile."

This is easy for me. I love all kinds of foods.

After dinner Mrs. Sakamoto brings a little tray with a stack of colorful squares to the table and sets one of them in front of me. She is a dainty lady, smaller even than Līhau. Sometimes I have trouble understanding her. She speaks only Japanese to her husband, and very little English to the rest of us.

"Candy," she says, showing me how to take off the first layer of paper wrapper. When I start to unwrap the second layer of what looks like cellophane she says, "No no, you eat."

"Really?" I have never seen a candy wrapper I can eat.

"Yes, special rice paper."

I'm pretty sure Mrs. Sakamoto said rice, but I look to her for advice. She smiles and nods ever so slightly, so I pop the candy in my mouth. She gives me a wink and sets the tray in the middle of the table. The tasteless cellophane melts on my tongue, exposing a fruity jelly candy. I'm lucky that Uncle offered to help the Sakamotos. Good smells and flavors, good people, these all make for good memories.

*   *   *

Summertime days come and go like the tides, high points and low points. Mostly fun times. Aunty Min has been gone almost everyday, leaving right after breakfast and home just before dinner. She always looks so tired that I don't expect storytelling time. When I ask, she says, "Don't worry about me. Family business got to be done, but people from that big town sure wear me out."

Today Aunty returns home from a trip with a bundle wrapped in brown paper.

"I run into that girl Kiana today, working at the mercantile where I buy my materials. She's a good girl, that one. Pretty, too. Helped me pick out some new patterns for your school clothes, Meli. Said this style is what the girls are wearing today. Come see."

Like summertime, Aunty Min's news has a high point, when she tells me Kiana helped her pick out dress patterns, and a low point, being

114

reminded that school will be starting in a few weeks.

Aunty notices my smile turn into a pout. "Well, here's something that should sweeten the end of your summer. Lopaka will be driving you over to Hilo tomorrow. You're invited to spend a few days with Kiana at her Uncle's."

"By myself?" I don't have to pretend I am surprised. This will be more of an adventure than I expected. When Kiana told me this secret at the end of school I didn't realize Aunty wasn't coming with me. On all the other trips to Hilo I have packed my clothes into a corner of Aunty's big faded yellow suitcase and slept on a cot in the corner of a bedroom I shared with her. This time I will stay in the city alone. Well, not alone, but without Aunty Min.

"Let's go up to the attic and find you a travel bag."

I follow her down the hall. She reaches for a knotted end of rope that hangs from the ceiling and tugs. A narrow door drops from above and half a ladder appears. She unfolds the other half, fastens the latch, and gives the stairs a shake. "You go first, Meli."

"I've never been up here." The steps creak as I climb up into the attic. I'm surprised how bright it is. There are two windows, one under each peak of the roof. An old lamp with dangly beads all round the shade catches the afternoon sun, scattering sunlight across the floor.

"Mind your head," Aunty Min warns as she straightens. "Stay under the ridge beam."

As short as I am, I have plenty of room between my head and the rafters, but a low ceiling doesn't matter anyway. The attic is almost full except for a clear path down the middle. Sheets are draped over mysterious objects tucked back against the wall. I pause at an old round-topped trunk. Since I've read plenty of books about pirates, I know trunks are filled with treasure. I stop while Aunty continues on her way toward the far window. The lid groans as I peek inside. No jewels or stacks of coins, just men's clothing, moth balls, and a bundle of newspaper clippings tied together with twine. I prop the lid open. The headline on the top sheaf is bold and ominous — Local Men Swept Away By West Coast Union. The picture is blurry. A crowd of people fills a big city street. A man is being dragged to a van by policemen with sticks. The caption print is tiny, with too many big words to understand. I start to thumb through the edge of the clippings to see if there are any more pictures. Here's another one, a close-up of a man between two policemen, but before I can read the caption Aunty Min scolds me from the other side of the attic.

"Nothing of yours in that trunk, Meli. Come and help out." Suitcases are balanced on top of a dresser and she teeters on a rickety chair as she reaches for a small brown one at the top of the stack. I run over to hold the chair before she climbs down.

"My first travel case." Her fingers trace across the dusty top. "You're a big girl, Meli, grown up enough to stay over in Hilo without me going along. This is about the right size for you."

"Thank you, Aunty." For the first time I will have my very own luggage, packed with just my things. I'm intrigued by the brass latches, and once I figure out how to pop them open I examine the inside. The case is lined with shiny polka-dot cloth. I explore the pockets and stretchy straps.

"You go on down to your room and pack what you want to take for play clothes. Set out your good pair of shoes and socks, and I'll fold a dress for church."

"Church?" The idea of shoes and socks in the summertime, even if I am going to be in the city, seems wrong.

"Unless he's fishing on Sunday, the proper thing would be for Kiana's Uncle to take her to church, and it would be right for you to join them."

"Okay." I know better than to argue with Aunty about church-going. I set the case at the top of the stairs. The ladder is steep, and climbing down is awkward. I stop halfway and reach as Aunty passes the suitcase to me. Back in my room I pull out my shoes. The socks I stuffed in the toes the last time I wore them seem clean enough to me. I use one of them to wipe the shoes off, setting them next to my bed. I sure hope my Sunday in Hilo will be spent fishing instead of dressing up.

The early morning fog matches my mood. Lopaka lifts my suitcase into the back of Uncle Kō's truck. As he opens the passenger door for me, I swallow a lump in my throat. I don't want Lopaka to see me cry, but I haven't been away from Aunty Min for a single night since mom left me behind. Tears fill my eyes. The first one breaks free and rolls down my cheek.

"Oh now, Honey Bee," she says, hugging me tight. "There's no reason to be sad."

"I know," I stammer and blurt, "but I already miss you."

"Before you know, you'll be back home." She pulls up a corner of her apron, wipes my face, and pinches my cheek. "Let's not keep Lopaka waiting."

Lopaka is checking the front tire, even though there's nothing wrong with the truck. He's just giving me a chance to dry my eyes. As we drive away, I hang out the window, waving until she disappears. For all the times I have been on a trip to Hilo, I have never felt so adrift.

"If what's in your head matches your face, you are far, far away." Lopaka says as he shifts into high gear and starts down the highway.

"Have you ever felt like your life was about to take a turn, but you didn't know if the change was going to be good or bad?"

"Yep." He winks at me. As we laugh, I feel a little more confident, and a little less *keiki*.

In a few hours we join the traffic along the waterfront. Lopaka toots the horn as he pulls over in front of a store. "There she is." He points to where Kiana is stepping out from the shade of a green and white striped awning.

"Aloha, Meli," Kiana greets me, opening my door. "My dad is already down at the boat, Lopaka. I've got this." She lifts my suitcase from the truck bed. "You have a safe trip," she says, closing the door and thumping the fender with the tips of her fingers.

"See you both in a couple days." Lopaka grins at Kiana. I wonder what they are up to, but I'll have to wait before asking questions. Kiana's legs are long, so I have to take an extra skip every couple of steps to keep up. We turn the corner and head up the hill away from the downtown toward her Uncle's house. She is describing a new recipe from a Ladies Club bulletin.

"I fixed this for our lunch. You know, like an experiment, I'll test this plate lunch out on us before I feed any to my Aunty and Uncle."

The mention of gobs of mayonnaise reminds me how hungry I am.

* * *

I wake in the middle of the night, and for some reason I can't fall back to sleep. Yesterday was my lucky day. We went fishing instead of dressing up for church. My good shoes are still wrapped in a piece of newspaper, tucked into the bottom of my travel case. Tomorrow is my last day in Hilo. No more nights on this lumpy cot. I tip-toe out of the room I share with Kiana and feel my way along the wall to the top of the stairs. A glow from the kitchen lights the stairway. Someone else is awake. I hear her humming an old Hawai'ian love song. When I reach the kitchen, a young woman is at the table. She glances up and smiles.

"Aloha, Meli. You can't sleep either?"

"No," I rub my eyes. "I need a drink of water."

"Here." She points to a full glass on the table, "I heard you coming."

I try not to stare as I slide into the chair, but I can't help myself. Her face is a perfect oval. She has shining eyes with dark lashes with wavy black hair covering her shoulders like a cape.

"Do you know that song I was singing, *'Awaiāulu*? Reminds me of your mother. You know, her beauty won many a heart, but only one true love."

A moment drifts by before her words shock me wide awake. The morning dream and Loloa's words from Kohala come back to me. This is the beautiful woman Pueo told me about, the one who can answer my question. I clear my throat. "You know my mother?"

"Yes, I knew your mother. Such a fine lady."

My heart starts to race as I ask. "Can you tell me where my mother is, and why she left me with Aunty Min?"

"Seems like just yesterday, but that couldn't be. Look how big you have grown. No one said anything about that night?"

"No. Why mom left is a story Aunty Min doesn't like to tell. She said the sugar business changed our family. How did sugarcane do that?"

"Your Aunty is right, but your mom will tell you all about that."

"I'll be seeing mom soon?" I set my glass down hard.

"Maybe soon, maybe later, but that's another story. You want to know why you got left with your Aunty?"

I nod and take a sip.

"Well, like Aunty said, families can change, and by that time it was just you and your mom. Lots of men around town thought your mom shouldn't be alone. She didn't pay them any attention. She worked hard to keep her job because she had a little girl to raise. A new foreman, Luna, was hired to oversee work at the warehouse. That's when the trouble started. Because he was so handsome, the women on our shift were trying to catch his eye, but not your mother. She just looked the other way. Then a loud-mouth woman named Lili was hired. Now that woman, she wanted Luna's attention for herself, but she couldn't figure out how to compete with your mom's beauty." The woman gazed at her entwined finger-tips.

This woman, Lili, reminds me of something Kiana said once, the first time she talked about her feelings for Lopaka. "You mean the green-eyed monster?"

She laughed softly. "More like a demon, Meli, because instead of love, her jealousy planted evil in her heart. Lili believed your mother secretly loved Luna, but that wasn't true. Your mother is a local born Hawai'ian girl. She had her own *'ohana*, her own family. She wasn't looking for anybody. Both Lili and Luna's people came to Hawai'i from the Azores, folks with different friends, different families. None of that occurred to Lili. The idea of your mother with Luna stuck in her head, drove Lili crazy. Her heart got so twisted she decided to get rid of your mother. She would trick people into believing a story, one that would hurt your *'ohana* and force your mother to run away."

"How can a story hurt someone?"

"People shouldn't care what we look like or where we come from. If we do what is good and right we can work together. But if a person is eager to hear bad news, all they need are a few dark words. Enough of that talk casts a shadow. People start to doubt your character, believe you are no good, and refuse to work with you. Do you understand?"

"I think so. Lili sounds like someone in Aunty Min's *mo'olelo* about Pueo. When the Ho'ololi first sailed, everyone was in harmony except this girl named Miki. She was always spreading dark words. After she betrayed the group, there was real trouble."

"Yes. That's how trouble happens. For your mom all it took was one night, one mistake, and one lie. Folks from work went into town to a dance hall. Everyone was having a good time. Then Luna showed up, grabbed your mom's hand, and didn't let go. He ignored all the women who wanted to dance with him. More than one lady sulked off. A few of the men grumbled until that woman, Lili, started to cut in. Every time a song began, Lili would whisper in Luna's ear, elbow your mom aside, and dance off with him. Fed up, your mom left the dancehall with a girlfriend. Lili followed them outside. She said she was sorry and asked for a ride. Your mom should have said no, but she was always giving people a third or fourth chance to do the right thing. They all piled into the front seat of your mom's car. She was driving, Lili sat in the middle, and her friend at the door. The road was narrow, and it was late. In the glow of the dashboard lights, right before they crossed a bridge, your mom looked over just as Lili reached across and opened the passenger door. A split second later, at the deepest part of the gulch, Lili shoved your mom's friend out the door, and dove after her into the darkness."

The woman stops talking. She is staring at my hands. My knuckles are white from the grip I have on my water glass. "Is this story too scary for you, Meli?" she asks in a gentle voice.

I manage to let go of the glass and put my hands in my lap. "Yes, but I'm okay."

"Alright. So, the car skidded to a stop. Your mom ran back down the road. In the dark she couldn't tell if she had gone too far or not far enough. She screamed for her friend, hoping to hear a moan, or at least a whimper. At first, the only sound was water gurgling in the stream. Far below a rock tumbled into the gulch. Then she heard a hollow thump like someone whacking a tree trunk with a heavy branch. She whimpered her friend's name one last time. Sure that Lili was climbing out of the ravine to kill her next, she stumbled back to the car. Instead of driving to the police station, your mom panicked and sped away."

"That must have been the mistake?" I ask.

"Yes, because as Lili limped back to town, she practiced the lie she had planned all along to tell the police. When Lili showed up at the police station, bruised and bleeding, she had even convinced herself that her story was true. She told the detective your mom had tried to kill her friends, all because of her passion for Luna. Lili described how she was the victim of a local woman's jealous rage. She was thankful to be alive, but she didn't think the Pilipino woman had been so lucky. After listening to Lili, the detective decided he was too busy to investigate a love spat. He sent two cops to follow-up on her story. From the back seat of the patrol car Lili guided them back to the bridge. In no time they found the other woman in the gulch, dead. The cops drove Lili back to town and started checking on her story. They drove to the dancehall and talked to the bartender. Then they drove out to the sugar mill to talk to Luna and his boss. One of the managers at the mill told the cops how your mom was mixed up with people who came to stir up trouble with the union. By the end of the day, the cops believed Lili. They blamed the murder on your mom. Before she showed up for her shift, a friend told her the cops were looking for her. Too scared to stand up for herself, your mom decided to run."

"But she didn't do anything wrong. Why did she abandon me?"

"She didn't abandon you, Meli. She decided to hide from the police, to disappear. And you needed to stay in school, to be with family. Aunty

Min never gave up on making things right. The detective said Aunty was wasting her time, but she finally found a lawyer who cleared your mom's name."

"Does that mean she can come home?"

"After the union trouble with your dad, too many bad memories linger in this place. I think she's waiting for you to go to her."

"Where?"

"O'ahu."

"In Honolulu?"

"No, but that's all you need to know for now. Time for bed."

"That's okay, I'm not sleepy." I try to stall, so I can learn more. "What's a union?"

"Union business is complicated. Enough talk for tonight, Meli."

"But, I don't even know your name."

"I'm Beatrice, Aunty Bea, honey. Now, off you go." she shoos me from the table like a chicken.

"*Mahalo nui loa*, Aunty Bea." I tip-toe upstairs. As I close the bedroom door, I wish I had given Aunty a hug. I'll remember tomorrow, first thing in the morning.

*   *   *

Kiana, Lopaka, and Sam are the only ones in the kitchen when I come down. Everyone else must have gone off to work.

"Sorry I slept in so late."

"Morning, Meli. You hungry?" Kiana asks, reaching for a plate in the cupboard.

"Yes, please. Didn't you catch any fish with Uncle Kō?"

"Lots of them, and we're already unloaded, sleepyhead." Lopaka winks at Kiana.

"He didn't mind waiting around for you." Sam chuckles, "Kō is down at the dock, said he had some cleaning up to do at the boat."

"Is Aunty Bea still here?" I ask, sliding into the same chair I used last night.

Lopaka's smile flattens as he sinks into the chair across from me.

"Nobody been visiting." Sam's face mirrors Lopaka's frown.

"I don't know anyone named Bea. What are you talking about, Meli?" Kiana asks.

Lopaka sucks air through his teeth before he asks, "Bea, as in Beatrice?"

"Yes, she sat right there." I point to his chair. Lopaka squirms and stands.

"I was careful not to wake you," I explain to Kiana. "I came downstairs for a glass of water."

"What did this woman look like?" Kiana scoots her chair closer and puts her hand on mine.

In this *'ohana* a room full of people is never this quiet, except when I mention my mom. I want to shout, 'She told me why mom ran away'. Instead I say, "Aunty Bea is a beautiful lady who knows my mom."

"Knew her," Lopaka offers softly.

"What do you mean?" A twist starts in my stomach. "Has something happened on O'ahu?"

"No Meli. Beatrice was your mom's good friend."

"I don't understand. Why are you talking about Aunty Bea that way?"

"Beatrice has a strong spirit, to return and share her story with you. You really don't know who she is?" Lopaka places his hands on the back of the empty chair like they are resting on someone's shoulders.

"No." I'm not sure I want to hear what Lopaka will say.

Sam stands at the kitchen sink with his back to us. Kiana is still holding my hand and gives me a squeeze. "I don't know Beatrice either. Why don't you tell us, Lopaka?"

"Beatrice has passed over."

"I remember Beatrice," Sam says, staring out the window. "Met her back when she worked at the warehouse. From the same island as my grandfather, back in the Philippines. I haven't thought about her for years." He smiles, then adds, "You are blessed with much aloha, Meli, for her ghost to appear as a radiant beauty."

"Weren't you scared, Meli," Kiana asks, "talking to a stranger in the middle of the night?"

"Remember back at the beginning of summer, when our family helped out at the Sakamoto's farm?" Even now, when I think of the owl's call, my skin goes prickly. "I didn't tell you everything. Pueo visited me in a dream, woke me up right before dawn. He said I would meet a beautiful woman in Hilo and learn about a journey. I couldn't sleep after that, so I went outside. My friend Loloa was sitting alone, out at the big table. When I told him about the dream, he said this woman would open the door to my future."

"Maybe Aunty Min kept your mother's trouble a secret because she trusted your *'aumakua* to take care of you." Lopaka says.

"You were visited by a ghost, Meli." Kiana pats my hand.

"Aunty Bea was the friend in mom's car that night?" I stammer as I look to Lopaka for an explanation.

"Yeah, Beatrice was murdered." Lopaka holds my gaze as I put the pieces together. "Do you want to know what happened to Lili?"

I nod, even though my ears are starting to ring.

"The sugar company knew how to keep the workers fighting each other instead of coming together. Lili's lies made it easy for the company to make more trouble for the workers. When the police questioned Luna, he lied. He bragged about your mom's wild love for him. Yes, she was jealous for his attention. No, next time she came in, he'd have to fire her. With your mom gone, Lili was sure that she had Luna for herself. At the next dance, in front of everyone, Luna rejected Lili. He boasted how he was too handsome for just one woman. Enraged at his insult, Lili grabbed for his throat. Their fight started a brawl in the dancehall, fists flying, bottles breaking. Turns out this was just the excuse the police had been waiting for. They came in swinging their clubs, so by the end of the night they had hauled the men who supported the union off to jail."

When he mentions unions I remember the stack of news clippings in the attic. The headline comes back to me as Lopaka continues.

"All along, Aunty Min knew the truth. She searched for a long time. Finally found a lawyer who believed her. He presented the facts to the prosecutor, and he agreed to drop the case. The last time I was on Oʻahu I tracked down your mom. When she heard the police weren't looking for her anymore, she said to bring you over, soon as we can."

"If Meli's mom is innocent, shouldn't the cops arrest Lili?" Kiana asks.

"Maybe they don't bother because it happened a long time ago, and Bea was Filapina and Lili is Portuguese."

"So, what?" Kiana surprises me as she spits out, "Doesn't make her a better person."

"No, but that's how the owners try to keep workers divided. Those days are ending." Sam says.

"The cops probably think Lili is harmless, prowling the alleys with her ratty hair and dirty dress, talking crazy talk," Lopaka says.

"Or the owners will use Lili again to stir things up," Sam says. "The problems at the docks aren't over."

"Tattoos?" Lopaka's description of Lili raises a frightening memory, blocking out what he said about my mom on O'ahu. "Does Lili have tattoos?"

"She does, but they're not marks of ancestors or *'aumakua*. She has black tears streaming down her cheeks."

"Oh, no," a lump in my throat feels like bony fingers choking me. "Down on the beach, at the canoe sheds. I tried to show Uncle Kō. A woman with tattooed tears yelled at me while I was cleaning the fish buckets. I couldn't make out a word, except my name. She knows my name!"

"Maybe you misunderstood her, Meli."

"No. Loloa scared her away, and he said she was talking *Pukikī.*"

"Portuguese?"

"Lopaka. Lili knows who I am!" I can see those tattooed tears and her mouth, twisted by anger, hissing my name. If Lili catches me alone again, I might not live long enough to make the trip to O'ahu. Trouble seems to visit some people more than others. The scariest moments of Bea's story come to mind.

"That was months ago, Meli." Kiana pats my hand. "Sorry to leave right now, but I have to go to work. See you in awhile."

Yesterday, Kiana had asked me to meet her at the mercantile store. I can't imagine walking there alone, past all those creepy downtown alleys. If only I could hide until Lopaka takes me home. I'm not a *keiki*, but with my elbows on the table and hands over my ears, I'm a long ways from feeling grown-up. Somewhere inside my head I hear Loloa, *No need to worry, just make a plan.* That's what I'll do. Even if Loloa said not to worry, I still have to avoid that crazy woman until I leave Hilo. Asking for a ride shouldn't be too obvious.

"Lopaka, are you busy? Just wondering...because..." This just might work. "Can you drive me to the Mercantile?"

"Yep, sure can." He winks at Kiana, and like sun breaking through a gloomy fog Kiana returns his smile. Sam chuckles and heads out the door. The mood in the kitchen lifts as I slip out from under the net Lili cast over me.

Lopaka picks me up before lunch. Instead of dropping me off, he parks and we walk cross the street hand-in-hand. As he pulls open the door to the store, a Japanese man pushes through.

"Excuse us." Lopaka pulls me out of the way and holds the door.

The man doesn't even say, *Thank you.* He glares at me, grunts, and shouts back at Kiana in a sharp voice, "You work. No play."

Kiana sits alone at the counter. Even though the door has slammed behind the rude man, she still whispers. "That's my boss."

"Well," Lopaka declares as he props his elbows on the counter, "we're here to keep you company. I'm thinking maybe you need a sweet."

Kiana gives me a wink. "Go ahead and look around Meli. Pick out a little something, a souvenir, my gift to you."

I don't mind being sent off in the store for two reasons. I had told Kiana a couple days ago that I wanted to buy something from the mercantile to celebrate my vacation trip. More importantly, Lopaka is flirting with Kiana, and I want to leave them alone. I wander up and down, poking into all the bins of fasteners and tools, rearranging the pots and pans, and running my hands along the bolts of colorful cloth. I end up at the back of the store, in the garden department. Rakes and shovels hang from the wall, boxes of axes, hatchets, and machetes of every shape and size are stacked on the floor. I turn the corner, starting down the last aisle where the shelves are filled with tiny garden tools for bonsai, little spools of copper wire, scissors and snippers, and stacks of stoneware dishes. At the end I come upon a shelf of tiny ceramic figurines for Oriental garden scenes. I am sure I will find my souvenir here among the pagodas and bridges, boats and fishing docks, men sitting with colorful robes and ladies with parasols. I decide on a pair of tiny white cranes. They stand on a polished pebble, their graceful necks bent to watch over their wings.

Just as I reach out, icy cold fingers wrap around my wrist. For a split second I am sure the hand belongs to the store owner who glared at me, but then I look up into a tear stained face. Lili raises a long handled hatchet and hisses, "Me-ehh-liii." She twists my arm behind my back and shoves me toward the back door.

"Let go!" I shriek. I'm kicking and fall down, but she drags me across the floor toward the open door. In a few more steps we'll be in the alley, and she'll hack me to pieces. My situation is hopeless. Nothing can stop her. Then I hear a shout. In an instant Loloa has one arm around me so tight I can't breathe and his other hand grabs the hatchet handle. As he wrestles with Lili, I am sure she will tear off my arm rather than let go. Loloa growls while he twists her hatchet-wielding arm backward. She howls like a kicked dog, and both of her hands fly open. The blade clatters to the floor at the same time Loloa spins free with me under his arm. Lili vanishes out the door just as Kiana comes running.

"You, let go of her," Kiana shouts at Loloa.

"Stay here, Meli," Loloa orders as he shoves me into Kiana and then runs into the alley after Lili.

"Are you hurt?" Kiana kneels next to me. "Who was that man?" She has me by the shoulders. "What was he trying to do to you?"

"Not him," I blubber. "It was…" I choke on my sobs. I can't say Lili's name.

Kiana turns me around. "Take your time, Meli." She brushes off my scuffed knees. "Tell me what happened."

"She was dragging me…uh…into the alley." Kiana smooths her fingers over the red welts when I show her my arm.

"And…" I gasp before I continue, "she had a hatchet." I point to the tool lying in the doorway.

"Who?"

I take a deep breath, but still can't control my voice as I stammer "Li…Li…Lili.

"Oh, Honey."

"Then Loloa grabbed her and wrestled me free. He scared her away."

"Don't cry, you're gonna be okay."

"I got out da door, and da alley all empty" Loloa is back, breathing hard. "She not on da street. Dat Lili, gone again."

"Who are you?" Kiana demands, trying to shield me from him.

"Just a friend, alright?" He smoothes back my hair and wipes a tear. "You okay, Meli?"

"Loloa." I snivel a couple times before I blurt, "How did you know I was here?"

"I been keepin' an eye on dat woman since da canoe shed. Speakin' of da eyes, you see my glasses?" Kiana points to where they poke out from under the shelf. "Good," he inspects the thick rims, "dey not broken." He settles the black frames on his nose. "Gotta help out my pal," Loloa pats my cheek, "so I'm gonna keep lookin'." He jumps out the door, but his hand still grips the jamb and he leans back in. "You take care of my friend, lady," he says, before disappearing into the alley.

Kiana stares after him, and finally asks. "Who is that, and how do you know him?"

"I met Loloa at Aunty's *hale* on a grown-up party night. I was lonely and went down to the old rock wall He just came walking up the path.

Remember? I told you, he's the one who came to Sakamoto's farm. Somehow he always shows up just when I need help."

"What an odd little man. I guess as long as he's watching out, lucky for you."

"I'm sorry Lili followed me here to your store, Kiana. I don't want to get you in trouble."

"Nothing broken." She says as she slips her hand into the pocket of her apron.

The bell on the front door chimes. "Where you girls hiding?" Lopaka hollers.

"We're in the back." Kiana calls to him as she bolts the alley door.

"What's going on here?"

"That crazy woman, Lili, just tried to snatch Meli," she says, returning the hatchet to the tool bin.

"Lili?" I hold still for Lopaka's inspection until he sees that, other than the shock of Lili's attack, there are only scratches and bruises.

"I don't have to tell my boss, do I?" Kiana asks as she straightens up the last few scattered items. "What happened was my fault. I forgot to lock the door when I took the trash out. He'll be furious."

"If the alley door had been locked, Lili would have come through the front. Don't blame yourself, Kiana." Lopaka steers us up the aisle to the counter. "You two wait for me here," he pauses at the door. "Gonna check around the block, make sure she's not hanging around."

"I'll sit on this, if that's okay." I slink behind the counter, pulling a wooden crate as far away from the front door as I can.

"That's fine. These are too hard anyway." Kiana wiggles on the tall metal stool next to the cash register. "You're a strong girl, Meli."

"I don't feel too brave right now."

"Well, you should. You make me think, I got no reason to be scared of my boss. Not locking the door was an accident. Anyway, there's a sign in the alley, 'No Trespassing.' Lili's the bad one, not me. I'm going to tell him what happened."

"Kiana, maybe you shouldn't say anything."

"Oh no, don't worry about me. Working at the Mercantile is a summer job, only a couple more weeks." Kiana laughs. "Anyway," she scowls, "Scary as Lili is, I need to do what's right to stop that crazy woman. I'll talk to my dad tonight. He'll know what to do."

The bell tinkles as the door swings open. I jump, ready to dive under the counter.

"Lopaka is back Meli, and wait 'til you see what he got for us."

"The long way around the block took me by Kakigori." Lopaka says as he hands me a shave ice.

"You must have run, this is barely melted." Kiana scoots the empty stool closer to her and pats an invitation for him.

Lopaka's eyes shine as Kiana shares an animated version of the fight at the back of the store. The story now includes the shouting and wrestling, and her racing back to witness my rescue, which isn't quite true, but that's okay. Kiana must have forgotten Loloa's name, because she calls him, "some guy." As I bite into the center of my cone, seeking the melting cream, I feel a tingly sensation. I know that Loloa is more than just a guy. He's my hero and I wish he was with me now.

*   *   *

At first I can't wait to tell Aunty Min about the trip. When I get to the last day, I don't know exactly how to start, mainly because Bea told me secrets Aunty Min had kept from me for years. The ghost story doesn't surprise her, but she starts pacing around the kitchen when I get to the part where Lili grabbed me at the Mercantile, so I leave out the details of the hatchet and spend extra time telling her how Loloa saved me from Lili. After she hears that Sam and Kiana went to the police to report Lili, she settles down and puts the kettle on the stove. I hesitate, wondering if I should ask Aunty Min about my mom on O'ahu. I bet this has something to do with the clippings in the attic trunk. I have so many questions, but the teapot starts to whistle for Aunty. She said we're going out to the *lānai*, and I don't want to ruin our afternoon.

I pull the pillows up and plop back on the pile as Aunty Min sinks back in her chair, her cup by her side. The mid-day breeze is gentle.

"A big city like Hilo is too busy for me. So many people." I stretch my arms out and embrace the peaceful surroundings. "I'm glad to be home with you."

"Well, you certainly had an adventure, and I missed you too, Meli."

"Is there time for Pueo's story?"

"Plenty of time before dinner. Do you remember where we stopped?"

"Lani was kidnapped. Pueo found the warrior's canoe and was leading the Ho'ololi to save Lani. The warriors stole all of her things, and one of them was about to whack Lani with her own hatchet. Pueo attacked just in time, and Lani dove into the ocean."

"Ah, the escape from the warrior's outrigger. The word for the tool the warrior raised against Lani was *koʻi*. The warrior had Lani's stone adze, not a hatchet. But you're right, Lani had lost everything, even the canoe from under her feet."

Overboard

Once Lani surfaced, her arms churned in powerful strokes that pulled her through the water. Someone had to be close behind, chasing her down. Her lungs burned. Any moment she knew she would be forced under by the grasp of a warrior or knocked out by the slap of a canoe blade. Exhaustion forced her to stop. She searched the water around her. Nothing. A swell lifted her high, and at first she didn't trust her eyes. She paddled in place and waited for the next swell to roll towards her. The warriors' canoe was paddling away. She had escaped! Her heart pounded in her ears as she gasped for air.

The thrill of freedom soon evaporated. Lani had never been alone in the deep blue. In a moment of panic she imagined herself at a threshold between the world of the air creatures and those of the water. She no longer felt afloat. The vast realm below was opening, trying to swallow her. Dizzy with the sensation of falling, she dog-paddled toward the sun, fighting to stay in her world. With each breath she thanked the gods for the blessings in her favor: the weather was balmy, the swells were rolling and spaced far apart, a light breeze blew, and plenty of daylight remained. She closed her eyes, tipped her head back, and was relieved to once again feel at ease on top of the water.

Pueo must have seen her leap from the canoe. He could direct her toward the Ho‘ololi. Lani opened her eyes, and spotted him, hovering above her. He swooped back and forth, squawking. She couldn't understand him. All she could do was wave. He flew a couple of loops on a path that must be pointing the way toward the Ho‘ololi. He circled back once more, and she waved again before beginning the slow process, hand over hand, of following Pueo.

*   *   *

Pueo rested on the pola. He had directed Ka'imi, so the Ho'ololi now sailed toward Lani. Even after several hours, she was miles away. Because Lani would need more than the sight of him to be encouraged to keep swimming, Pueo asked a favor of Ka'imi.

"Ka'imi, Lani needs water. Gourds in bag."

Ka'imi soon returned with two sealed gourds tied together with a cord. "Grasp this loop. When you drop the gourds, the empty one will float so the water gourd won't sink."

Pueo struggled as he took off, almost snagging one of the gourds on the pola rail. Each previous flight between the canoe and Lani had been shorter, but this trip took much longer. The gourd of fresh water weighed almost as much as he did. If his pace varied, his cargo started swinging, pulling him back and forth. Afraid that he would lose his grip, he clutched the skinny cord tighter. His talons cramped and his wings ached. Pueo aimed at a splash in the ocean. Soon he would be able to drop his package.

*   *   *

Lani raised her head high above the water. A land creature left to swim in the open water for too long can lose sense of direction and time. Had minutes or hours passed since Pueo's last visit? She began to doubt that she still swam in the right direction. Fatigue clouded her thinking. The ocean had changed. The wind chopped across the surface. The rolling long swells lifted her up-up-up, then dropped her down-down-down. She no longer held back her tears. She had spit out so much salt water that her tears tasted like fresh water. This only made her sob more. She had never been so thirsty. Flat bottomed clouds shuffled across the sky. None were dark enough to bring rain. At least they brought shade. She rolled over and started crawling again, stroke after stroke, hoping she was still on course to the Ho'ololi. A movement caught her eye. Was that him? She stopped swimming, treading water again, waiting as she rose up the crest of the swell to take a better look.

Only a few predators in the ocean reveal themselves as they hunt at the surface. Lani spotted what looked like shark fins cutting the water. In an instant she lost sight of them as she dropped down in the trough. From where she floated, in the lowest point, her horizon was less than a hundred feet in all directions. She had seen small sharks swimming

132

at the edge of the reef, and even bigger ones in the deep blue when she was fishing with Ka'imi. A *manō* had even bumped their canoe once. She didn't want to be nudged without a thick plank of wood between her and the blunt-nosed beasts. The next swell passed by, and this time nothing cut above the water. She sank back down as the swell rolled on. In a few seconds she would face whatever creatures approached. She took in a deep breath so she would float as high as possible, and curled into a ball. As they swam closer, Lani bobbed on the surface, hoping they would just swim on by.

"*Nai'a!*" Lani exhaled and scissor-kicked her feet.

A pod of dolphins surrounded her. Nai'a jumped and dove along the white-capped swell. A young one approached and poked her shoulder with its smooth snout, turning her to see Pueo approach. The gourds splashed in front of her. She marked Pueo's path across the sky, but she didn't need to. As he wheeled and flew away towards the Ho'ololi, the dolphins turned and followed. A young one stayed with her, while the rest chased and jumped through the swells in the general direction Pueo had disappeared.

She reached out for Pueo's gift. One gourd bobbed high, the other floated just below the surface. She shook the top one. Nothing? She pulled at the heavier gourd, shook it, and heard gurgling. Lani pried the lid off and sipped the sweet water. With shade from the clouds and her dolphin companions her spirit rose and lit her face.

Pueo's package had buoyed more than Lani's spirits. After drinking the water, she had pressed the wooden disc back against the sticky rim, sealing the empty gourd. She wrapped the cord around her waist and the empty gourds bounced and bumped her ribs as she swam. At first this created an amusing rhythm and she was distracted. The novelty wore off as the hours passed. The cycle of swimming, floating, and then swimming again strained Lani to her physical limit. She struggled to keep her mind clear. Even staying afloat required too much effort. She tied a knot in the cord to bring the gourds close together, slipped them behind her neck, and wrapped the long end of the cord around her hand for safe-keeping. This makeshift pillow kept her face above the water. Her arms and legs sank like waterlogged branches. The *nai'a* stayed close and kept nudging her gently back to the surface.

Lani tipped her chin toward the sky and rested. The sun hovered above the gold bands of clouds on the horizon. When the stars came out tonight, she would cross over to the heavens and fulfill the name her father gave her, Hokulani. The gift of a name was important to her people. If Kekoa had a family name, maybe he could have joined the crew of the Hoʻololi. That would have changed everything. Kekoa had certainly lived up to the name the fisherman gave him so many years ago. How courageous of him to go to Kāulamana, profess his love, and accept Pueo's form. How brave to have followed the Hoʻololi across the open ocean, just to be with her. How fearless his attack on the warrior. Those few seconds of surprise gave her time to escape. Pueo had flown all day to keep her and the canoe on course. Now she floated alone while he rested on the Hoʻololi, waiting for the bone changing. The dolphins remained close. They would provide companionship when darkness closed in. Afraid this was her last sunset, Lani prayed that her love would make her strong and the stars would guide her toward morning. A dolphin's caress reassured her, and Lani sank against the smooth skin.

"*Naiʻa*," she patted the side of her friend. "Look."

In the last rays of the sun Lani gave in to exhaustion, sure that the gods were playing a final trick. They had sent the spirit of Pueo, skimming along just above the water, to check on her one last time. She hugged the gourds to her chest and lifted her head. Yes, Pueo flew toward her, with dolphins leaping on either side.

When the sun fell from the sky, so did Pueo. With a cry, "La-aaa-nii-ii," he plunged into the water.

"Kekoa," she called out, keeping her eyes on the spot where he had disappeared. How long did the change take? She couldn't remember. What if he sank too deep, or his lungs didn't hold enough air?

"*Naiʻa*. Help him!"

*   *   *

As Kekoa sank in the darkness, he regretted wasting his last breath to call her name. He flailed his arms, seeking the light above. The water bubbled around him. He felt the press of a *naiʻa*, lifting him toward the surface and tossing him into the air. In a few swift strokes he was at Lani's side. Still gasping, he lifted her up and smothered her salty sunburned face with kisses.

"*Naiʻa, mahalo nui loa*," he thanked the dolphin as he draped Lani's arms around his neck. "Lani, let me carry you." He wanted her to hold his shoulders so he could breast stroke with her at his back, but she slipped away at his first powerful kick. He tucked one arm under hers and cupped her chin in his hand. She fell limp in Kekoa's hold, clutching her gourds with one hand and gripping his arm with the other.

Using a side-stroke Kekoa tried swimming again. Towing Lani along was like swimming with a *keiki*. His hip bumped her back with every kick. The feeling raised memories from long ago when he was rescued from the rock. Once the darkness surrounded them, he longed to hear Lani tell him the names of the *hōkū* as they popped into the sky one by one. Watching the stars was one of their favorite evening games, but not tonight. Kekoa swam on, following the *nai'a* as if in a dream.

"How far?" she croaked, breaking the trance.

Wavelets splashed Kekoa's face as he answered.

"Ho'ololi is close..."

"Where?"

"*Nai'a* knows the way...They'll find us."

"It's dark," she whimpered.

"Torches...Lani...Please...Stop talking."

Kekoa stopped often to scan the horizon. The crew would never see their small dark heads bobbing in the water. He must spot the torches and gain their attention. His impatience to catch sight of the canoe drained away his energy. He fought against a creeping doubt. The Ho'ololi could appear before the moon rose, or he might have to swim late into the night. The odds were against them. Kekoa began singing a *keiki* counting song in his head, hoping the familiar tune would distract him.

He sang each number, one to ten; *'ekahi, 'elua, 'ekolu, 'ehā, 'elima, 'eono, 'ehiku, 'ewaluā, 'eiwa, 'umi*. As he sang the first verse, he decided to repeat this simple song before rewarding himself with a look around. To count to *lau*, a very large number, should take a long time. He hoped that the Ho'ololi's torches would appear by then. If not he would start over. He would sing all night if he had to.

Kekoa ended the first counting cycle and rolled onto his back. Lani still clutched the gourds to her chest, which made floating easier for him. He rested while the dolphins splashed nearby, their fins faintly dappled by the starlight. Startled by the sound of the conch shell horn, Kekoa raised his head. The most beautiful sight, the Ho'ololi, hovered so close the torches illuminated her sails.

*   *   *

As twilight had faded, Ka'imi had told Ikaika part of Pueo's plan. The spirit bird would not return to the canoe that night, but Kele should continue to follow the path where Pueo had last disappeared. Once the darkness of night hid the horizon, they should light torches to help him guide Lani to the canoe. When the moon rose, Ka'imi would begin to signal with his conch horn. His *pū'oleolē* would call out, "voo-hoooo."

On the leeward bow three men held torches high, a cluster of fire while others circled around them, guarding against wayward sparks. Ka'imi sat on the windward bow, to search the dimly lit half circle that reached out ahead of the canoe into the night.

Lifting the *pū'oleolē*, to his lips, Ka'imi blew a short blast and listened as the sound faded away.

Ka'imi heard a voice in the darkness. He cupped both hands behind his ears. Yes, that was Kekoa, hollering. "Here! *'Ei'a*. Over here!"

Ka'imi called out, "*I laila*, there at that place," to direct Kele toward Kekoa's shouts. The sails swung over and the Ho'ololi turned. The circle of torch light reached out and sparkled on the water where Lani floated.

Ka'imi continued to point, "*I laila*." The crew began chanting along with him. They dropped the sails and glided directly toward Lani. Everyone without a torch rushed to the forward rail of the *pola*. Several already clung to lines, leaning out from the center of the top rail, ready to grab for Lani as she drifted toward the space between the hulls.

No one could see Kekoa. Only Ka'imi could hear him. He must be next to Lani, but where? Ka'imi would have one chance to save Kekoa. With every eye focused on Lani nobody noticed as Ka'imi moved toward the hull, fastened a line to a post on the *pola*, knotted the end, and threw it over the side. The knot skipped along on the top of the water. Ka'imi grabbed another line, hooked his leg around the post, and swung down as close as he could to the water. He could no longer hear Kekoa over the shouts of the crew.

Ka'imi frantically searched for an odd ripple, or an out-of-place wave, any movement that would reveal Kekoa's location. Just before the crew lifted Lani to the *pola*, the gourds left her hand. Instead of floating away, they rose above the water. As Ka'imi stretched down toward the hovering gourds, Kekoa kicked hard and reached up. Ka'imi felt an arm slip through his hand. He squeezed tight, determined to hold on.

In the excitement of pulling Lani aboard the men pushed, shoved, and crowded around her. No one witnessed Ka'imi grappling with his invisible catch. Kekoa had grabbed the knotted line and hung on while Ka'imi searched for his other arm, and hauled Kekoa onto the *pola*. With Kekoa's full weight on his shoulders Ka'imi shuffled toward the stern seat. He had saved the young man who had rescued his Lani.

Once Kekoa was safely tucked away in the sleeping space, Ka'imi ran back to the *pola*. He pushed past the crew members huddled around Lani. Dropping to his knees, he scooped up her limp body and hugged her to his chest. The crew pressed against them, shouting questions.

"What about Miki and Lapa'au?"

"Did they swim with you Lani?"

"Are you the only one who survived?"

Worried that the warriors lurked nearby, the men at the bow doused all but one of their torches before running to the *pola*.

"How close are the warriors?" The last torch bearer asked as he cast a circle of light around Lani.

Bagged like a sack of taro, almost murdered, fried by the sun, and pickled by the ocean, Lani was bruised, sunburned, dehydrated, cold, famished, and barely alive. Ka'imi, drained from the tension of the chase, cradled Lani to protect her from the jostling of the curious crew. He searched for Ikaika and caught his eye. Pointing his chin towards the stern, Ka'imi signaled his intent. Ikaika easily lifted Lani from Ka'imi's arms, and Kele helped Ka'imi to his feet.

"Stay here and douse that torch," Ikaika growled at the crew.

He carried Lani to Ka'imi's sleeping place, followed by Kele and Ka'imi. Huddled in the darkness, the crew speculated on the events of the previous night. Their questions would go unanswered, perhaps for days.

"She needs to drink before she sleeps." Kele had cracked a coconut and drizzled the water into a cup. Ka'imi gently pulled Lani to slump against him. He tipped the gourd to her lips. At the taste of the scented water she gulped and spit up. After smaller sips of the nourishing liquid her stomach began to settle. Ka'imi leaned in close and pushed her salt encrusted hair back from her ear so only she could hear.

"Rest Lani. Kekoa sleeps safely behind you."

Those few words were sweet medicine. Relieved that Kekoa was safe and soothed by familiar surroundings, she fell asleep to a lullaby of familiar voices coming from the stern seat where Ka'imi, Kele, and Ikaika sat talking.

Winged Bounty

K a'imi stayed by Lani's side. She slept fitfully, waking only to ask about Pueo or to drink a little coconut water. Pueo did not fly from the *manu* that day. Hiding in the bottom of the hull, he dozed or sat at the gap in the mat, peering in to watch Lani sleeping. After the previous day's events the crew grew ever more curious about the owl. Lani's rescue added to their murmurs. Speaking to Pueo would only feed the men's gossip, so Ka'imi avoided him. An unsettled mood of magic surrounded the canoe.

The next morning brought a steady rain. To Ka'imi, the wet owl was a miserable sight. He propped a paddle against the stern seat and draped a mat over the shaft. While Pueo huddled under his little shelter, everyone else frolicked in the rain. Tight woven mats funneled streams of fresh water into gourds. Ka'imi carried Lani out to the pola and washed the salt from her scalp. He rubbed a nourishing mix of oils and flower extracts through her hair and gently over her sunburned skin. The sensation of someone washing her hair, the sweet smell of the soothing oils, and the simple act of being nurtured by a loved one, revived Lani. He wrapped a soft *kapa* around her shoulders and carried her back to the stern. She fell into a deep sleep and didn't wake for hours. When Ka'imi offered her a full gourd of water, she drank in long, slow swigs.

Testing her voice, Lani whispered, "I'm starved."

"Good to hear because I soaked some banana in coconut water while you slept. Should be soft by now." Ka'imi held on as she grabbed for the bowl. "Don't eat too fast," he warned.

Lani grew stronger every day, but she still stayed behind the mats in the shade. Sleep did not come easily. At night her dreams replayed the worst parts of the kidnapping, Miki's taunting laughter and the tattooed welts on the warrior's chin. Those memories played over and over again.

Every afternoon Ikaika sat with Ka'imi at the stern seat. They exchanged idle chat or reminisced, but never spoke of the events that led up to the night of the kidnapping. On the third day after Lani's rescue Ikaika said, "Lani has spoken to you of the others?"

"No."

"It is time for us to know."

"I will ask." Ka'imi leaned down and spoke through a gap in the mat, "Lani, Ikaika would speak with you."

She nodded and slid the mat aside.

Ikaika moved down from the seat, eased himself to the hull floor, and held her dark eyes in his.

"Lani, I must know what happened to Miki and Lapa'au."

She coughed softly and chose her words carefully. In spite of Miki's betrayal, she didn't want to say outright that Miki had schemed with Short-One to help the warriors take her from the Ho'ololi. Even though Lapa'au seemed to move freely on the warrior canoe, Lani didn't want to suggest that she was part of the plot. To tell Ikaika details of the fight she had with Miki on the canoe was impossible. Just thinking of Miki's words made Lani angry. Miki and the warriors were in the past. The further away from those people and those feelings that Lani sailed, the better.

"I don't know, I think they'll be safe. I was the only one causing trouble."

Ikaika raised an eyebrow and looked over to judge Ka'imi's reaction. Ka'imi shrugged and looked away.

"Will they come after the Ho'ololi again?"

"No, they have what they want. And they certainly don't want someone like me."

Even with cracked lips she managed a grin. She had stood up for herself against the warriors and was encircled with *aloha*, by people who loved her.

Ikaika heard the truth hiding behind the words Lani spoke. Miki and Lapa'au were willing captives. He hoisted himself off the hull floor and returned to his place on the seat next to Ka'imi.

"You know, Ka'imi, with Miki and Lapa'au gone, settling your island will be impossible."

"I agree, our plan has failed."

"No, we have not failed, but a village based on one woman, no matter how strong she is, can't last. Lani and a few of us could remain while the rest of the crew return home for more women and supplies. I know hardship and danger will be faced, both for those who stay on the island and those who return home. I still expect to raise your island, Ka'imi."

"I have seen a different ending to our voyage, in a vision just five days ago before the warriors appeared." Ka'imi paused before he continued. Ikaika would resist what he was about to say. Ka'imi's vision did not match Ikaika's desires. "The Ho'ololi turned away from the island, leaving no people behind. I council you to follow what the goddess has shown me. We should sail north. Kele will follow the star song and learn the path that leads to the island. Then we all will return home. The next trip will go easier."

"I am reluctant to follow your advice." Ikaika's gaze lingered on Lani as he rose. "I will speak first with Kele and Maloka."

*   *   *

Lani returned to her day-to-day activities on the canoe. Concerned that she lacked the strength to haul in a big catch by herself, Ikaika asked Maloka to help her. At the beginning of the voyage Maloka was sure that Ikaika would pick him to be fisherman. Surprised with the honor of captain of the watch, he couldn't reject Ikaika's offer, but Maloka still believed he was the best fisherman. At first he was skeptical of Lani's abilities on the canoe, but after her swim to freedom he was eager for any excuse to be close to her. As each line slipped over the edge, hand over hand, he watched out of the corner of his eye as Lani fixed the next lure. Although Lani and Maloka worked well together, for some reason the fish weren't biting.

Kele called out a greeting as he approached Ka'imi and Ikaika on the stern seat. Ka'imi was distracted watching Maloka and Lani at the *pola* rail, so Ikaika answered for him.

"These winds are a blessing, Kele," Ikaika invited him to join them, "they speed us towards Ka'imi's island."

"Not just the winds are in our favor, the swells are rising as well." Kele sat down, thumping Ka'imi on the back to bring his attention to the their conversation. "The weather is changing."

"Pueo has mentioned the same. Are we ready for a storm?" Ka'imi asked Ikaika.

"The hull caulking is tight, but the lashings are worn. One plank has almost worked free. I will set the crew to work before we fall apart."

Whitecaps tossed the surface and the Ho'ololi ran with a strong wind. While Lani and Maloka continued to send their lines into the water, the rest of the crew started to check and repair every lashing. The deck of boards and poles allowed the Ho'ololi to flex over the waves. The gaps between the planks let the sea splash through instead of lifting her hulls out of the water, but weeks of sailing had loosened the *pola* structure. The crew worked all morning, tying new cords at each junction where poles and planks met. Ikaika wanted to reward their hard work.

"Mākaukau, can you make a special meal for tonight?"

"I can crack open a couple gourds, soak some yam and banana. A meal, but only dried food." Mākaukau brandished a lid off and shook a small basket under Ikaika's nose. A few shriveled fish rattled in the bottom. "A feast means fresh, and I can't serve up what don't want to be caught."

"Let's give the day a chance to bring us fish before you break into the yams."

Nai'a still escorted the Ho'ololi. A few raced along next to the hulls, but most trailed behind. Lani spotted them jumping in the distance. Soon the patch of ocean between the dolphins started to bubble and froth. The pod must have found a school of fish. The boiling water marked where the underwater cloud of fish broke the surface. She recalled an old saying; where little fish swim, big fish follow.

"Oh, we should be lucky like those dolphins. They are feasting on our dinner," Lani sighed.

"Why only fish to eat? There's talk we might soon settle the island. We should eat *pua'a* to celebrate," Maloka leered. "Thinking of pit steamed pork makes me hungry." He laughed as he mimed the tusks of a boar with his fist at his mouth, his thumb and pinky poking out to the sides.

His comment about the island disturbed Lani. She remembered the intensity of Ikaika's eyes, burning into hers as he asked about the other women. Although Ikaika had agreed to her father's council, she was sure his heart was pushing him to ignore Ka'imi's advice. Ikaika wanted to settle the island. She could see the passion in his eyes. Maloka was wearing that same face now. The two most powerful men on the canoe had come to some agreement. What if Kāulamana's magic didn't release Kekoa? She didn't want to consider that future. And even then, he couldn't compete against these men.

"Lani, are you listening to me?" Maloka's voice broke through.

"Yes, of course," she lied. "What did you say?"

"Why not cook a piglet?"

"If Mākaukau had a big stone bowl he could build a fire, but we only have wood platters and *kukui* lamps." As she spoke, the answer seemed obvious to Lani, but apparently not to Maloka. "And a piglet certainly wouldn't provide the crew with more than a small bite. Anyway, there's not enough dry fuel to build a cooking fire." Maloka's hungry stare turned quizzical and Lani realized that this powerful warrior was not too clever. Self-assured she declared, "So Maloka, I guess the pigs are safe from your stomach for now."

He laughed at their misfortune, and she joined in.

A shadow flitted across the *pola* as Pueo returned to the *manu* and hopped to where Ka'imi lounged. Like the rest of the crew, Lani only heard hoots and chattering from Pueo. How unfair that after all they had been through only her father could talk to the bird. As Pueo flew off, Ka'imi crossed the *pola* and spoke to Ikaika. Orders were called and the sails shifted slightly. The Ho'ololi turned to follow Pueo.

"I wonder what Ka'imi's bird has seen?" Maloka asked.

"We'll find out soon; he hasn't gone far." Lani wondered if the bright sunlight was creating a mirage on the ocean. Not only did the surface sparkle, but also the air above flashed with a thousand twinkling lights.

Ikaika called for the sails to be dropped. As they drifted closer the mystery was solved. They were gliding into a school of flying fish. Frightened by an unseen predator below, shimmering *mālolo* filled the air. A layer of silver wriggling creatures soon covered every surface of the Ho'ololi. Their gossamer red-veined fins, efficient in propelling them into flight out of the water, were now useless wings.

"You're off the hook, Maloka." Lani slapped his shoulder as she ran off.

Everybody grabbed a basket and joined in the frantic harvest. Mākaukau pulled an empty gourd from storage. The crew scurried and slipped across the *pola* and along the hulls, gathering their gift from the sea. Once the gourd was overflowing, he started to clean and chop, fixing bowls for a feast.

High spirits filled the crew of the Hoʻololi. First, they were blessed by an abundance of *mālolo* that had leaped from the sea into their waiting baskets. Next came the news that Pueo had spotted a flock of birds. The crew cheered as they passed over the Hoʻololi. Coastal birds meant land was nearby. Mākaukau served up trays of seasoned flying fish and yams, lightly flavored with a newly opened gourd of *kukui* nut seasoning. Several coconuts were cracked open and passed around, adding to their merriment. Drums, rattles, and shakers filled the air with rhythm. Voices harmonized in song, and colorful jokes were followed by waves of laughter.

Late into the night the crew ate their fill and spoke of the prospect of raising the island tomorrow. Lani had slipped back to the stern with a bundle of food for Kekoa. Foremost in her mind was how she and Kekoa could stay together. She had to warn him about the plans both Ikaika and Maloka had for her, though she didn't want to alarm him with her fears.

"Has Kaʻimi talked to you about his recent vision for the island?" she asked as she slid the mat closed.

"He said the Hoʻololi turned away."

"Yes, but did he say if we settled the island?"

"In the doldrum vision his original dream was unfulfilled. No landfall, and no people left to settle the island. That is why he counseled Ikaika not to split the crew."

"Have you heard anything different since then?"

"I'm never close enough to the crew to listen in. Why?"

"I'm trying to figure out how you and I can stay behind, together. Are you sure that Kāulamana's magic will release you once we land?"

"Pueo follows the Hoʻololi. Once we are on the island, I won't need the owl. I'm sure Kaʻimi's island will break Kāulamana's spell."

"What if Ikaika doesn't take my father's counsel?"

"I can't imagine Ikaika ignoring your father."

"Yes, that's true, but..." Lani swallowed. You didn't see the fire in Ikaika's eyes. Those words never left her mouth. She waited to see what Kekoa would say next.

"Lani, if we stay behind, won't we be going against your father?"

"Oh, ..." In all the worry about who would end up settling the island,

Lani hadn't considered what Ka'imi expected of her. Determined not to be held back from her dream of being with Kekoa, she made up her mind.

"We have to stay, Kekoa, even if Ka'imi and Ikaika decide the Ho'ololi will return to the village. Before the canoe leaves the island, I will tell Ka'imi of my desire to stay with you. I will ask what he sees in our future. Then I will ask my father to go to Ikaika on our behalf."

"Ka'imi must convince Ikaika to help us." Kekoa said. "We need the pigs, and all of the seeds, plants, root stock, and tools set ashore."

"Of course." She paused, reluctant to admit that depending on Ikaika's blessing was unrealistic, but she could not speak of failure. "Anyway, we would see them all again soon. Ikaika could lead a new crew, my father could return with them next season on the Ho'ololi with more people and provisions." As they cuddled under the stern shelf, the celebration on the *pola* continued to fill the night with music. They were quiet, each busy with thoughts of the future.

"Promise me one thing, Kekoa. If Ikaika decides to split the crew once we reach shore, no matter what, you and I must sneak away."

"I promise," Kekoa agreed absentmindedly. He was busy building their homestead. Raising a *hale* meant hauling rocks, chopping down trees, dragging poles, twisting rope, and lashing a framework together. Months of hard and potentially dangerous work lay ahead, but Kekoa was confident. He had discovered the thrill of following his passion. Lani's excitement was contagious. He was in love.

Taking his promise as a vow, Lani imagined building a family with Kekoa, not considering the hardships they faced. Life in her *hale* would be comfortable. They would sleep on mats she wove and eat from bowls she carved. She imagined Kekoa out in the garden as he tended taro, sweet potato, and gourds. *'Ulu* twigs stuck in the ground grew into stately breadfruit trees. Their *hale* would be built at the mouth of a valley and overlook a bay protected by a reef. There they would fish, collect seaweed, and swim in the sparkling aqua water. And everywhere, lots of chubby, cheerful *keiki* ran about. This was her dream.

"The land is so close, I can almost smell the earth. After all this time on the Ho'ololi I'll be waddling for days before I can walk straight." Lani said. "Imagine sifting the warm sand between our toes."

"Never mind the sand, I'll just be happy to have my own toes all day!

Let's sleep. Tomorrow I'm flying north to find a landing place for the canoe."

"I see lightning on the horizon, you'd better pull the mat tight." She poked him with one last tease of the day. "Don't get your feathers wet tomorrow."

The Storm

Pueo slipped from behind the mat. Even in the protected bottom of the hull the wind ruffled his feathers. Sails slapped, lines strained, and the masts creaked as they came about. Only a few words Ikaika shouted to the captain of the watch were clear. The rest were caught by the wind and flung away.

"Run ahead... squall... tie down..."

In these conditions those commands told Pueo more than enough. He hopped up on the seat to share his plan with Ka'imi.

"Huge storm."

"I hope the island will still take our bait," Ka'imi joked nervously.

"Will hook the island today."

"Ikaika must stay ahead of those," Ka'imi gestured with his chin towards the horizon. Black clouds loomed on the southern horizon. An ominous sound like drums pounded in the heavens and rumbled from the roiling wall.

A gust buffeted them. Pueo scrambled, failed to stay upright on the slick wood, and slid sideways into Ka'imi.

"Talons worthless," he righted himself and clawed away from Ka'imi's thigh. "Don't need to..." Pueo's yellow eyes searched Ka'imi's.

Ka'imi finished the words for him. "Tell me to watch out for Lani? I've been doing that her whole life," he laughed. "Go now Pueo, we'll be fine."

Pueo flew just before the rain came in sheets. The crew labored under the press of the storm. Ikaika called for a double watch to handle the sails with three men to brace the steering paddle. They lashed a safety net of lines they could grab to keep from being washed overboard, stowed away provisions, and tied down gear. Lani worked her way forward to check the sow and her piglets under the bow. Crammed together at the back of their stinky pen, their beady eyes stared at Lani, their ears quivering.

"Don't worry, little piggies. You're my future. I'll be watching out so nothing happens to you." She tossed in a treat of rotten papaya before she re-tied the latch-pin on the pen door.

All morning the Hoʻololi raced ahead of the storm. Squalls boiled past them, but the foreboding wall of the storm stayed behind. The wind whipped up the waves. The height of the swells tested the skill of the crew and the worthiness of their vessel as they surfed up one side and careened down the other. Sailing a bucking boat was adventurous in the daylight, but could become a treacherous ordeal at night. Ikaika wasn't sure how they would manage once the sun set. He chanted a prayer, asking for the storm to release them.

Kaʻimi was first to hail the island, a white tipped mountain rising above the wind swept waves. The crew's initial cheer shifted into jubilant shouts that competed with the howl of the wind.

Hooked, they reeled their island up from the sea. Their faces beamed at the sight. The smell of land fed a hunger to feel new earth beneath their feet. As they neared the southern tip of the island, the snout of another island appeared beyond the first. All were eager at the prospect of more islands. Everyone continued to search the horizon except Ikaika and Kele.

The ocean rarely forgives mistakes. Earlier, as they worked to outrun the fury of the storm, Ikaika had urged the winds to turn away. Unfortunately his prayer was answered, but the timing was wrong. As the storm swung around to follow the sun so did the winds. The pressing winds released them, blocked by the towering mountains. The storm waves were now a more powerful force, pushing the Hoʻololi toward the west shore of the island. Ikaika signaled to Kele. He shook his head. The cliffs were too close. They would never clear the first turn they needed to catch the northeast winds.

As the Hoʻololi sped past looming red cliffs the rest of the crew realized their situation. The direction of the storm swells would not change as fast as the winds had. Influenced by a thousand miles of open ocean, the huge waves still pulsed northward. They faced a leeward shore without a wind to fill their sails.

Ikaika ordered the crew to coax the canoe to sail north. Lines were set. All hands worked to keep the fickle wind in their sail. Ikaika stood with Kele, directing the men at the steering paddle.

"If we can reach that point before dark..." he gestured to a black finger of land far up the coast. Ikaika worried that a strong current must run between these islands. Without a way to control the canoe, they would be swept along by the storm swells into this channel. "We must find the wind."

*   *   *

With the mind of a boy in the body of an owl, Pueo had lifted off from the stern bench that morning, unprepared for stormy conditions. A gust buffeted from above and pushed him down to the foam-tossed tops of rising waves. Struggling to stay dry, he worked to gain altitude. The next few moments tested all of his skills as he raced to escape the dangerous winds. Once he cleared the turbulence he settled into an easier, long distance pace.

Approaching from the south, he passed over cliffs where the slopes of the island broke free from the deep blue ocean. Two radiant peaks shone white in the sunshine. From high above the ocean, Pueo took in the vast archipelago, its islands shrouded in clouds faded off to the northwest. Although the peaks of Hiva Oa were grand, what looked like the tallest mountain in the world rose before him.

As soon as Pueo reached the southern tip of the big island, he soared down to land on a grassy promontory. A full cycle of the moon had passed since he felt land beneath him. He scratched the earth with his beak and nibbled on the plants. He rubbed his face against a tuft of grass and then remembered his human obligations. Without food or other offering, he sent up to the heavens a most sincere prayer in thanks to Hina for guiding them across the ocean to this beautiful land. She had provided generously for her people.

Lifting off, he began a low, silent flight across the plain in search of some unwary bird pecking about, far from the safety of the trees. Soon Pueo flew up a ridge of the mountain, a ground dove dangling from his talons. Perched on a jagged outcrop he tore into his catch, glancing at the landscape between bites. A forested slope rose steadily ahead of him. Curious for a closer look at the white topped mountain, Pueo finished his meal so he could explore. As he climbed higher up, the forest grew stunted and scraggly. The plants thinned, scattered across rocky slopes, their shapes became spiky or twisted before they disappeared altogether.

Almost at the mountain top, he hovered above a patch of mysterious sparkly white. Landing on a bare patch of cinder gravel a few feet away he approached cautiously. His head bobbed side-to-side. Sparkly white was like nothing he had seen before. Not coral or sand, the gleaming hummock looked like the purest sea foam frozen in time. He took tentative steps forward, blinking at the brilliance. The sunlight glinted off the surface in tiny rainbows. Standing a wingspan away he scrutinized the sparkly white before, with a single flap, he hopped on top of the mound. As soon as he landed, a piercing cold shot through his feet, colder than any mountain spring or stream pool in the shadows.

He pecked the surface and pieces broke off and scattered. He picked up a chunk. The sparkly white magically changed from solid to liquid in his mouth, a most unusual drink of water. This certainly was a magical gift from the gods. Flying onward over bizarre shapes and endless fields of sparkly white, he turned away from the peak and soared south, back to the familiar forest green and black rock lowlands.

He landed on top of a dead tree, a perch with a sweeping vista. This island was growing. A cratered peak steamed. A mountain ridge pocked with vents spewed rocks and ash. Incandescent rivers oozed from cracks in the earth. Lava flowed like mud down the flank of the mountain, the molten rock exploding wherever it touched the sea, cooled into tortured shapes with a hiss of steam and gases. Flying south again down the mountain slope he felt the spirit of the land, vibrant with abundance. Fertile soil, streams, forests, tool stone, and all along the long coastline, lines of waves broke over coral reefs, no doubt teeming with fish. A flock of shore birds passed below him and he wondered if the Hoʻololi was approaching the south point. Exploring would have to wait. Tomorrow, he and Lani could wander the island together.

Ashore

Pueo urgently retraced his flight back to the southern tip of the island. He was relieved to see the wall clouds of the storm churning away to the southwest. The outer bands of rain had weakened and were not reaching the island, but the ocean swells still surged and high waves crested. He flew to the rocky point where he had first landed, and sat out of the wind in the shelter of a scrubby bush. Scanning the sea, he finally spotted the Ho'ololi. She had already sailed past the cliffs of the south point, much further north than he expected.

He flew along the shore until he found a tree overlooking the ocean. He settled on a high branch and watched as the Ho'ololi raced up and over the swells. They were heading for the channel between the two islands, the sails set to catch as much wind as possible. Pueo's thoughts whirled like the dry grasses below him. Ikaika was trying to clear the far point and sail past the island. Pueo flew on, chasing her up the coast.

Most of the shore was inhospitable cliff and crag. This island was too young for broad sweeping beaches. To land the canoe in these conditions would be almost impossible. As he hovered over the next rocky overlook, he noticed a subtle change in the canoe's course. Had they lost the wind? No, the sails were full. They still surfed down the waves, but now they seemed to be sliding sideways quicker than they were making headway. The channel current was bending the swells. Each wave was pushing them a little closer to the island. From his earlier flight Pueo knew that only a few bays embraced protected coves. He flew on, searching for a beach where the Ho'ololi could make safe landing.

His next perch was in a wind-swept tree at the end of an ancient lava flow. High surf crashed against the rocks below him. Misty spray peeled from the top of the waves breaking on the outer reef, sending a hazy fog inland. Entering this bay was impossible. The reef lay unbroken just below the surface without any gaps wide enough for both her hulls to clear.

He lifted up from the branch, hovered above the headland, and watched with dismay as the Hoʻololi continued side-slipping. With a stronger wind the canoe should have been able to turn and set a course a safer distance from the shore, but right now nothing seemed to be in her favor. He flew on to check the next inlet, hoping for a safe entry.

Pueo flew slowly, barely skimming above the ground. The sun had disappeared behind the wall of storm clouds hours ago. So far, he had followed the Hoʻololi along the rugged coast effortlessly. Once he took his human form, he would be forced to follow the canoe on foot. Stumbling barefoot over jagged rocks to the next bay would take hours. A dark despair began to smother him. For lack of a better plan, Pueo flew back toward the canoe.

The wind shifted, the sails sagged, and the Hoʻololi drifted towards shore. The steering paddles no longer held them on course against the approaching waves and they started to crab sideways. The danger of capsizing loomed closer with each steep wave. Now they could hear the roar of the surf, the break marked the shallow water where rock and coral lurked just below the surface. The teeth of the reef could tear them apart. Ikaika commanded the crew to secure themselves, but the boom of the surf drowned out his voice.

At this moment everyone knew they were on their own. Although Lani, Ikaika, and Pueo prepared for the worst, each one had a different idea of what was most important.

*   *   *

Horrified that the pigs might drown, Lani struggled across the *pola* towards their pen as the Hoʻololi surfed down the face of the swell. Water surged up through the planks and swirled around her knees. If the canoe smashed to pieces on the reef, she wanted the *puaʻa* to have a fighting chance to swim with the rest of them. She dropped into the hull as the canoe pitched over and clawed her way to the bow while the canoe surfed toward the reef. When the canoe hovered at the top of the next wave, Lani had both hands on the gate pin, ready to free the pigs.

The Hoʻololi wallowed and Ikaika feared they would *huli*, flip over. Water sloshed in the bottom of both hulls. The men had stopped bailing long before Ikaika shouted for the crew to prepare for impact. The canoe started to climb the next wave, but an invisible hand seemed to hold her back. As the Hoʻololi trembled without moving forward, Ikaika wrapped his arm tight to a line wound around the mast. He must not go overboard when they slammed into the reef.

Pueo hovered above the canoe. He tried to match the pace of the Hoʻololi and grasp the broad line on the *manu* as the hull rose up to meet him. Missed it! The Hoʻololi dropped away. He fought to stay above the tail of the canoe. She raced up the next wave and teetered over the crest. This time he connected. Sinking his talons into the twisted fiber of the line, he fought a powerful instinct to spread his wings and let go as the canoe fell away. Managing to keep his grip, he rode along as the canoe surfed the next wave. He couldn't see Lani, but in the dim light he found Kaʻimi, his focus intent on the opposite bow. Pueo followed Kaʻimi's stare and spotted Lani on the far bow, pulling desperately on the gate pin. Pueo clung to the *manu*, wondering what to do as the canoe rose high on the wave. At the crest he decided to let loose, his wings lifting him high above the top of the mast. The Hoʻololi fell on the reef with a sickening thud. Kaʻimi was thrown to the bottom of the hull. Men cried out as they dangled from lines or slammed into wood.

The last big wave of the storm was a rogue. Combined with the current of the channel and the turning of the high tide, the water heaved the Hoʻololi up and wedged her on the outer edge of the reef. The following set never matched that monster wave. The Hoʻololi teetered, then settled where she landed. Ikaika released his grip and hurried to check both hulls. The Hoʻololi had survived intact. The canoe stuck solidly on the reef, her bow pointed toward the beach. The waves rushed past the hulls. They were in no immediate danger of capsizing or sinking. In the confusion he called for those who could move about to check for injured crew.

Most of the men suffered contusions and concussions, except for Mākaukau, who had a severed finger, cut clean away by a line breaking free and running out. Ikaika searched the canoe. No Lani. Just before the wreck he had called to her as she crossed the *pola* and dropped into the far hull. He had looked away to secure his line to the mast. He never saw her again.

"Quiet!" Ikaika thundered, his powerful voice cut through the shouts and commotion. "Lani is missing." For a moment only the roar of the surf filled the silence.

"Who was the last to see her?"

Nothing but blank stares and shaking heads.

"Where's Ka'imi?"

"Knocked out cold." Kele called from the hull.

Ikaika ran to Ka'imi's limp body. "Ka'imi!" He shook him by the shoulders. "Can you hear me?"

Delirious, Ka'imi called out, "Lani?"

"No Ka'imi, it's Ikaika. Where's Lani?"

"At the pigs." Ka'imi touched his forehead where an egg sized lump throbbed and saw a twin for each worried face around him.

Black clouds to the west hastened twilight. The surf-generated mist made the surrounding ocean visible in feet, not yards. Ikaika could only see the open ocean behind them. The spray flying from the back side of the waves as they broke across the reef hid the bay. He resisted the urge to leap over the side to search for Lani. Most of his crew had injuries. If he dove in now, others were sure to follow. Swimming in unfamiliar waters in the dark invited trouble. More men might be lost.

And so an agonizing night began not only for Ka'imi, but also for Ikaika. Ka'imi had always been his close friend and companion. Since the earliest preparations for the voyage of the Ho'ololi Ikaika had envisioned joining their families. When they reached the new land, he had hoped to take Lani as his wife, if she would have him. He had never spoken of his feelings for her, and now he feared his desires had been silenced by the sea. A chill settled over him.

*   *   *

When the Ho'ololi slammed onto the reef Lani had both hands on the gate pin. The latch was stuck, so she had braced both feet against the bottom rail of the gate and pulled with all her might. The impact broke her grip. Like a coiled spring she launched into the air. She screamed as she flew overboard, but no one heard her cry over the deafening blow of the Ho'ololi striking the reef.

Only Pueo, from high above the mast, had witnessed Lani hurled from the bow. He had not seen where she hit the water or where she

154

surfaced. He flew along the outside of the reef to check the rough waters. Searching back and forth between the white capped swells turned up nothing. Maybe she cleared the reef. The surge might have pushed her towards shore. He skirted along the breaking face of the waves, scouring the churning white foam that rolled toward the shore. If she was unconscious, every second counted. Where was she?

Swooping back toward the reef, he spotted Lani, face down in the bay. Frantic, Pueo pleaded for the sun to set. He must change into Kekoa to save her. He plummeted out of the sky, only to hover above her limp form with no idea what to do. In desperation he sunk his talons into her shoulder. Surely she would respond to the pain. Nothing. Hooking both feet into her tangled hair he grabbed her head, flying sideways as he struggled to lift her face from the water.

The next swell caught her arm. As Pueo thrashed just inches above the whitecaps, she rolled slightly, but he was no match for her weight. Common sense told him to let go, to abandon her, yet he could not give up. He continued to flap, his wings beat against the water as she sank. With his talons still entwined in her hair, the ocean wrapped around his feathers and she pulled him under. Drifting down toward the bottom, Pueo stretched a wing toward her face with one last thought. At least we are together.

Kekoa took in a lungful of salt water. Shocked to consciousness, he flailed and pushed off from the bottom, a hank of Lani's hair still wound in one hand. Surfacing behind the shore break, he kicked hard to make the next wave and kept kicking until they tumbled with the foam up onto the beach.

Kekoa dragged Lani feet first up to dry sand, rolled her onto her stomach, and began pumping his fists against her ribs, trying to force the water from her lungs.

"Breathe, Lani, breathe," he sobbed as first sea water, and then spit, vomit, and frothy bubbles flowed from her mouth.

Lani lingered within the tenuous space between life and death while Kekoa toiled to bring her back. That moment seemed eternal, until Lani gagged, wheezed, and gasped for air.

Her skin was cold and clammy like a dead fish. She needed to be warmed. He carried her from the sand up into the cliffs above the high tide line. A little warmth from the day radiated from the black rocks, and the boulders offered protection from the wind and spray.

With Lani safely tucked away he went looking for shelter. Nearby he found a low ledge with a dry floor. He carried her up the hill, rolled her to the back of the shelter, and wriggled in. Holding her tight, his will for Lani to survive burned like a flame. The heat from within Kekoa spread from his heart to hers.

Seeking

Strange even magical events occur between the land and the sea. The next morning dawned as if there had never been a storm. The high tide returned at sunrise and lifted the Ho'ololi off the reef, undamaged. Her sails unfurled, the canoe drifted just outside the bay, waiting for Ikaika's next orders. From the bow, the crew scanned the shore, but still no sign of Lani. If she swam to land and survived the night, why wasn't she on the beach looking for them?

"I must search for Lani," Ka'imi pleaded, "but I need help."

"I will go," Ikaika replied, "and Maloka and Kele will help us."

They lowered themselves one at a time off the *pola*, timing the swell to carry them over the sharp edge of the reef. They started their search along the high tide line below the rocks.

"Over here," Ka'imi called. As they jogged toward him, he seemed to crumple. By the time they reached him, he sprawled on the sand.

"Ka'imi, are you feeling alright?" Ikaika asked as he placed a hand on his shoulder. The lump on Ka'imi's forehead was beginning to turn purple.

"Yes, I'm fine, just a little dizzy." Ka'imi pointed to a spot above where he sat. "Be careful or you'll erase her tracks," he shouted as Kele ran up the hill.

"Scuff marks and one set of footprints," Kele shouted, "here between these rocks."

"Rest Ka'imi, we'll find her," Ikaika said. He joined the other two, and they followed the footprints halfway up the hill. They jumped rock to rock and circled around, returning to where Ka'imi sprawled on the sand.

"Why did she walk up into the rocks like that, only to come back down to the beach?" Ikaika asked.

"Maybe she was looking to see if anyone else washed ashore," Maloka offered.

"You may have missed a turn, she might have wandered into the next gully. Let's follow the tracks again." Ka'imi suggested as he raised himself to his elbows and accepted Kele and Ikaika's help to stand.

Ka'imi moved slowly while the other three were impatient and soon disappeared over the hill. Shuffling along, Ka'imi recalled the words Kekoa used to describe his first night alone after Kāulamana's spell was cast. After the change he had slept under a rock. So, at every potential shelter Ka'imi stopped to peer into the shadows until he found what he was looking for. On his hands and knees Ka'imi ducked under a rock ledge and wriggled on his stomach to the back wall. He crawled back out and sat. His legs dangled over the opening. He gently pulled a loose thread from the small bundle in his lap while he waited for the others to return.

"This is where she spent the night." He held up Lani's tattered *kīhei*.

"I have heard of such a thing. A person chilled in the water feels a burning fever and they shed their shawl," Kele said.

"She could be stumbling in a daze, lost." Ikaika left at a jog, followed by Maloka and Kele.

Ka'imi sat on the rock. "I will wait here, my head is aching."

He listened as they called out for Lani. Their voices faded until they disappeared over the ridge. Once they were gone, Ka'imi jumped down to examine a patch of ground at the edge of the shelter. When he retrieved Lani's cape, patterns in the fine sand caught his eye. Now that he was alone, he could examine the marks. The scratched lines in the sand were the tracks of an owl. Pueo was with Lani. Kāulamana's magic was still at work. Ka'imi broke off a tuft of dried shrub and walked back down to to where he sat earlier, just above the high water line. After he first found the tracks, he had distracted the others on purpose by pointing out the footprints above, high in the rocks. Otherwise how could he have explained away what the sand clearly showed. Someone unconscious had been pulled from the water. Ka'imi had reclined across the imprint of Lani's body, hiding the place where Kekoa had worked to save her life, his knee prints drilled into the sand at her side. When he had pointed out the footprints leading away from the beach, the men had run up into the rocks. They were moving too fast to notice how these footprints were deep in the heel compared to the others. Ka'imi had seen where Kekoa carried Lani, left her while he searched for a shelter, and then returned to move her to where they slept. He would keep the discovery of the owl tracks under the rock to himself. Ka'imi wasn't ready to explain that part of the story to the others. He finished sweeping with his crude broom. Nothing from last night remained on the beach. He walked back up to the ledge where they had left him and resumed his perch.

After a while Ikaika and the others came back down the hill.

"We lost her tracks in the rocky ground above. We climbed to all the high spots and searched many of the gulches." Ikaika's face sagged, a heavy sadness in his voice. "No trace of Lani."

"If she was strong enough to walk away from the beach, where is she?" Maloka asked.

"I fear the spirits are at work around us. We can do nothing more. Please, help me back to the canoe." Ka'imi feigned weakness in order to persuade the others to give up the search. But his concern was real. Lani was lost to the magic of the big island.

*   *   *

Indeed, like tendrils of a vanishing mist a powerful magic had drifted through the rocks that morning, long before the search party had come ashore. At the first hint of dawn Kekoa awakened to the faint warmth of Lani's skin pressing against him. She had survived the night! Without waking her, he rolled away and wiggled to the opening. Crouching low, just in case someone aboard the canoe was scanning the hillside, he climbed to the top of the ridge. He sat with his back against a boulder where he had a view of the coastline both north and south. The sweet smell of wet earth mixed with the tang of the ocean. How much time would they have before Ikaika began the search for them? He hoped Ka'imi would be among those who came ashore. Kekoa could describe their plan if he and Lani stood side-by-side, together on the island. He smiled.

"Imagine the look on Ikaika's face as I stand before him." Kekoa spoke softly. His magical appearance would have to convince Ikaika to agree. The sun shone on the highest point of the island peak across the channel. As the light crept down the slope to greet the water he shuddered.

His feathers sprouted.

"No! Not right," he yowled. "This is not what Kāulamana promised. I've been tricked!" He heard a yelp from the rock ledge far below.

A sickening taste in his mouth reminded him of his vow to Kāulamana. He had agreed to do anything to be with Lani. In seeking the island he had done his best to protect her from harm. They had reached land. He had fulfilled his side of the bargain, and Kāulamana had kept her promise. They could be together forever. She never said anything about being a human. He landed in front of the shelter and walked into the shadow until he could see Lani crouching against the back wall.

"Come on Lani, walk toward me so you can stand up."

She shook her head.

"You have to move. Feel your weight and balance your body."

She snapped at him and lifted one foot, flexing the talons before touching them back down.

"That's good. Don't be nervous. Maybe just move both feet."

She snapped again, this time moving the other foot.

"That's right, baby steps."

She rocked back and forth, and lifted her feet, moving side to side.

"You're learning a lot faster than I did."

Lani glared and snapped her beak at him with a series of rapid clicks.

Kekoa wanted to tell Lani how graceful she was, nothing like the panic fit he threw his first morning. Instead he blurted, "I can't believe how cute you are." In a blink, he had to dodge sideways as she jumped forward and snapped at his face.

"Okay, I deserved that," He moved out from under the rock and paced back and forth in the sand at the front of their shelter. "You need to stretch your wings." In the distance he heard plovers call to each other down on the beach.

"You can talk to me if you just relax." He waited until she stepped toward the sunlight. "I don't know how the words come out. Kāulamana said to speak from your heart."

Stopping under the lip of the rock, she tilted her head and searched his face.

"Kekoa?"

"Lani," he rushed forward and nuzzled her beak with his.

"What happened to us?" she asked, pulling away.

"I don't know."

"Why an owl?"

"Better an owl than Kolea."

Lani glared. Not wanting to lose any feathers, he backed away. "I'm sorry." With a hop he perched on the rock across from her. "Teasing used to be fun. Please don't be mad."

"I am mad, but not at you. I'm mad at Kāulamana. We should be humans!"

"Maybe being an owl is better."

"But why change me? Why couldn't you be a boy again?"

"At least we're owls at the same time. We have the whole day ahead of us, and who knows what will happen tonight."

"I want us to be humans, right now." She stomped her foot in the sand and almost fell over.

"Lani. You are missing from the canoe. Ka'imi and the others will search for you. If you were a girl, how could you ignore your father's call? You would go to him, at least to let him know you were alive."

"I don't want to agree, but you're right." More than pleasing her father, Lani remembered the other problems with having a human body. "Neither one of them would agree to leave all the provisions so we could settle the island. No matter how much we argued, they would force us to return home."

"Our love will survive on this island, even if we're owls." He nodded and spread his wings.

Startled by the truth in his words, she strode toward him through the fine sand in front of the ledge. She hopped up onto a small rock outside of the shelter and ruffled her feathers.

"Then teach me how to fly."

*   *   *

For Ka'imi the voyage had gone far beyond his dream. Under Ikaika's leadership and Kele's guidance the Ho'ololi had not only fulfilled Hina's star song, they had fished up two islands. The possibility of these islands would be a lure for future voyagers. Unexpected tragedy had awaited them as well, taking away any chance of starting a new village. The disappearance of Lani and Kekoa saddened his heart. Ka'imi hoped they were safe and, if the gods were willing, he would see them again someday. Maybe his people would return to settle here and raise their families in peace.

A breeze blew from the northeast that morning, bringing the scent of trees in bloom and rain from the clouds that hung over the mountains. As the crew prepared to furl the sails, Ka'imi sensed the power of the goddess shimmer in the air. His instincts told him that Lani and Kekoa were alive, but how could he explain Lani's fate to Ikaika?

"We should wait, just a while longer." Ka'imi reached out, touching Ikaika gently on his forearm. "Take a moment to place the beauty of this land in your heart before we leave." He didn't know what else to say. Clouds lifted off the peaks revealing her new cape of white. Mist swirled behind the hills and curtains of rain fell to the north. If only he had proof, something more than the landscape to share with Ikaika.

Ka'imi spotted two birds flying high above the grassy bluff beyond the cove. Finding joy in their playfulness, he pointed them out to Ikaika. They wheeled and tumbled, and turned toward the bay.

As the first bird approached the Ho'ololi, the second bird wheeled back and hovered at the reef. Ka'imi wondered if these were land or sea birds. These were owls! Ka'imi recognized Pueo as he flew over the mast. Was Kāulamana's spell still at work? As the second owl approached the Ho'ololi, he heard her speak, "Forgive me father."

An ache tore at his heart. His wife must still be consorting with the goddess. With Hina's favors Kāulamana still wielded her powerful magic. He had been used to serve the purpose of the goddess, again. Hina had given him the dreams, the visions of the land that rose from the sea, but she had sent Kāulamana to sing the star song. Hina's island was for others who would come in the future. The stars Hina had strewn across the sky had planted the seed. And as for love, Kāulamana had meddled and stirred that bowl as well. Ikaika's desire was not true love. Kāulamana had nudged Kekoa, the one who pledged his righteous love for Lani, to choose her path that night. She had protected her daughter throughout the journey. With her powers, his wife held the veil open around him now.

"A vision surrounds me that explains Lani's disappearance," Ka'imi said as he turned to Ikaika. "She has been called by the goddess and is with the 'aumakua."

Ikaika draped his arm across Ka'imi's shoulders as he followed the flight of the Pueo. "I am stuck in this world Ka'imi. My eyes are stones compared to yours. If only I could join in your vision of the owls."

When he spoke those words, Kāulamana heard true love radiating from Ikaika's heart. She broadened the shimmering magic, sliding the veil around Ikaika as well. In awe he felt the rush of her magic and the freedom of flying with Lani and the *ʻaumakua*. What an honor to take part in this farewell with his old friend, Kaʻimi. What a relief to know Lani was not lost. With much *aloha*, he let Lani go and the veil fell away.

Ikaika rubbed his eyes as he stepped away from Kaʻimi. Only the closest crew members heard his soft voice command, "Raise the sails."

Kaʻimi stared as the owls wheeled one last time above the Hoʻololi before flying back toward land. For everyone, returning home was *pono*, the right choice. Kekoa and Lani were together, even if they were owls. The flame of love in Kaʻimi's heart grew bright as he raised his arms to chant his farewell.

"*Aloha ʻoe...Aloha kākou...Mālama aloha...*"

Aloha

My jaw drops open. A silent "What?" sits ready to fall from the tip of my tongue.

"Now, honey," Aunty Min adjusts her dress and takes a sip of tea. "Close your mouth dear before a moth flies in."

"But Aunty," I stammer, "why didn't the magic end? Why wasn't Kekoa a boy again?"

"Meli, you know the tales about the first people on our islands. Lani and Kekoa were not those people, they couldn't be. And as you travel the islands you might hear other tales about Pueo, but this story is the one that was given to me."

"Then why did Lani have to become an owl?"

"Because they were in love and it was right for them to be together. You remember your Sunday School lessons, the Bible story of Noah and the Ark. It takes two!"

I chew on that one for a moment. "But didn't Ka'imi know what was going to happen? Why didn't he stop Kāulamana?"

"Life is full of unexpected changes sweetheart. Sometimes we think we know what we want, or what is best for other people. Life doesn't work that way. The true power of happiness is seeking *aloha* where we are, not where we think it will be." She pauses.

"And love is always with us if we carry it here." She taps her fingers over her heart and then, leaning forward, holds out her arms for me.

*   *   *

The whole family crowds around the kitchen table after dinner to talk about my journey. I am surprised to find out that I'm not just sailing to Oʻahu. Mom and I are going to the Mainland! Uncle Kō and Lopaka are making a run to Honolulu next week, taking me and a few other passengers over to the docks where the freighters leave for California. Mom will meet us at the pier with the tickets, and we will sail on a ship called the SS Manoa from Honolulu to San Francisco. Instead of sad talk, everyone is excited about the preparations for my voyage.

"I can help you with Meli's dresses Min." Aunty Līhau offers. "She's going to need different clothes for San Francisco."

"We'll have to sew long sleeves on all those dresses." Aunty Min stands behind me and measures the length of my skinny arm with her hands.

"I hear the weather is chilly, Meli, like upcountry on the north side of Mauna Kea," Lopaka says. "Cold and wet."

"Meli will need a winter jacket, Min, and some trousers for the trip over." Uncle Kō says.

"Cotton cloth won't do. She needs something thick and warm. There's a wool blanket rolled up in the hall closet."

"The one with the green and yellow stripes?" I don't want to seem ungrateful, but does Aunty Min know how silly I will look in a travel suit stitched together from that scratchy blanket?

"My old wool peacoat is tucked away in a trunk up in the attic. You cut that up, Min. Should be plenty of material." We all laugh, because a coat big enough for Uncle Kō has yards of cloth. I am relieved that my suit will be dark navy blue.

"Tomorrow we'll go through the attic, Kō. You and Lopaka bring down the stoutest trunk. We'll start sewing and packing."

*   *   *

And that's about how fast everything happened. The Aunties spent a few days adding sleeves to my dresses, ripping old jackets apart, and sewing my new travel clothes. I used that time to say my goodbyes. Tomorrow I sail for Oʻahu, so today I have a bunch of little things to do. At breakfast I made Lopaka promise to tell Kiana that once I had an address I would send her a postcard and that I expected her to write back. I was too embarrassed to tell Lopaka he should marry her someday. By the time I get back I will be much older. I'll tell him then.

I walk down to the old stone wall to say *aloha* to the owls. I say a prayer, just to make sure that I will see my ʻohana again, especially Aunty Min. As I sit looking over the pasture, the one person I'm missing and I'll probably never see again is Loloa. A dark gray cloud forms across the ocean and drifts toward the valley. The rain falls like my tears as I remember seeing him for the first time from this rock perch. I know everything happens for a reason, but I have a hard time weighing the excitement of joining my mother and traveling to the Mainland against the sorrow of losing not just a friend, but what might be my first love.

I leave the pasture behind and climb the stairs to where Aunty Min sits on the bench by the kitchen door. She cradles a small box on her lap.

"Your dad started sending his letters here to our address because once your mom ran away, he didn't know where she lived." She sets aside a stack of letters tied with a ribbon. "But every once in awhile he sent a few postcards and pictures to me."

We spend the last hour of daylight going through his letters to Aunty Min, and I learn a little more about my family. She still doesn't say much about my dad and that Union trouble. Between what Beatrice told me and what I'm hearing now, the newspaper clippings in the attic start to make a little more sense. She passes me a few loose pictures of my father and his brothers. Apparently those uncles have lived in California for a long time. The most recent picture of my dad was taken at the beginning of this summer. A group of young men are standing with their arms wrapped around each other. People fill the background, and some are taking pictures of their friends and families. Behind them is a huge bridge, cables rise into the sky and disappear in the distance. I turn the photo over. On the back there are words written in soft pencil.

"I like a bridge — It breathes romance;
There's new adventure on the further side
And I will help you cross."

Tiny printing across the bottom reads. "Pedestrian Day - May 28, 1937. Poem by W. Rose, read by Gov. Merriam at the dedication of the Golden Gate Bridge."

"I'm sure your dad meant to put this poem in his last letter to your mom," Aunty Min slips the photo under the ribbon and settles the lid on the box. "Don't pack these in your trunk, Meli." She hands the box to me. "Put them in the bottom of your knapsack, and hold tight to your bag. Don't set it down. Give her the box as soon as you are settled on the ship to California."

Lopaka picks me up early in the morning. There are no tears when I leave Aunty Min this time, all of those were wrung out last night. Today is only *alohas* because I will see them all again, someday. When we get to Māhukona, Lopaka parks the truck as close as possible to the dock. Uncle Kō is starting up the engines of his big fishing boat. Black smoke puffs are quickly swirled away by the breeze. Lopaka drags my trunk up the ramp and across the deck to where three others are tied down behind the wheel house. I guess the rest of the passengers are below, so I sling my knapsack over my shoulder and head to the aft rail to watch Lopaka loose the lines before he leaps across. We are underway.

The day is perfect, sunshine and puffy clouds. No chance of a storm delaying our trip. Lopaka says we should be in sight of the harbor before nightfall. I watch the hem of my dress, the only sleeveless one I own, flutter around my knees. The blue and green pattern looks like the sparkling sea, and a matching bow holds my hair back from my face. Above the chugga-chug sounds of the engine I hear a familiar voice and look toward the bow This can't be true!

"*Hūi*, Meli."

"Loloa, what are you doing on Uncle's boat? I thought you never went out on the water."

"Yeah, dat was da old Loloa." He cleans the salt mist from his glasses with a corner of his shirt, before settling them back on his nose. "Just like you, da new Loloa is ready for adventure."

Author's Epilogue

This story about Pueo is not a Hawai'ian cultural tale. The natural history of the Pacific Ocean islands is a vast landscape and the cultures of the people who call these islands home is diverse. There are attributes we all share in common, a strong sense of family, the importance of teaching our children respect, doing what is right, and the need to work together as a community. It is by honoring these values that people of all cultures, and the environment that nourishes us, might survive the challenges of growth, industrialization, and technology.

The voyagers of the South Pacific built seaworthy canoes, capable of making trips of over 2,000 miles. They navigated by reading the sun, the moon and the stars, the clouds, ocean swells, land birds, every clue that nature provides. By the time European explorers entered the Pacific Ocean in the 1700s, almost all of the habitable islands were already settled by these skilled voyagers.

The art of navigating long distances across the deep ocean using the stars was almost lost to Polynesian people. The Polynesian Voyaging Society (PVS) worked hard to preserve this aspect of their cultural heritage by building voyaging canoes and learning wayfinding from Master Navigator Mau Piailug, a Micronesian from Satawal, Yap. He was willing to teach them the skills needed to sail along the ancient roads across the dark-blue waters without instruments. The Ho'ololi in Hooked by the Stars was inspired by a modern voyaging canoe, the Hōkūle'a, built by the PVS in 1974. The Hōkūle'a is 62 feet long, with double hulls and a beam of over 17 feet. In 2014 the Hōkūle'a began the World Wide Voyage, a three year journey to circumnavigate the earth on a mission of education and collaboration for a sustainable "Island Earth." On July 4, 2016 she was at Woods Hole Oceanographic Institute in Massachusetts. Hawai'i celebrated her historic homecoming at Magic Island, O'ahu, on June 17, 2017.

Voyagers from the southern Hiva Islands (later colonized by Europeans and named the Marquesas) may have been the first people to settle

Hawai'i, landing somewhere near the south point of Hawai'i Island. In addition to some shared material culture, this association is suggested by similarity in language. More than half of their basic words are shared. Hawai'ian words and phrases are used throughout the book, to remind the reader that this is a living language, spoken on Hawai'ian television and radio, and in homes, work, and schools. The earliest settlers were followed by voyagers from Tahiti, then other Pacific Islanders. When people sailed on long voyages, they took plants and animals along with them, to establish gardens and survive in unknown lands. Lani's sweet treats have been a favorite of islanders for a long time. Chewing sweet cane is believed to have begun in the islands around Java about 6,000 years ago.

Stone quarries on volcanic islands in the Pacific have basalt that can be geochemically sourced. Craftsmen in ancient workshops made tools from material from the quarries. Archaeologists map the trade of these tools. The tiny island of 'Eiao, one of the northernmost islands in the Marquesas Archipelago, has a unique fine grained basalt. Archaeologists excavating in the Republic of Kiribati on Tabuaeran, (also called the Line Islands because of their location on the Equator), found a small adze (similar to the *ko'i* Lani lost to the warriors), made from basalt that was sourced to the quarry on 'Eiao. 'Eiao is over 1,300 miles southeast of Tabuaeran. In honor of this association the Wild-One speaks a few words of Kiribati.

The doldrums refer to sailing conditions in an area of unpredictable winds that straddle either side the equator. Without the winds, sailing vessels drift with the currents. North of the equator the prevailing winds blow from northeast to southwest. South of the equator the prevailing winds blow from southwest to northeast. Sailing with a strong wind filling the sails, a voyaging canoe can travel over a hundred miles in a day. The imaginary Ho'ololi followed the same route sailed in 1995 by six modern voyaging canoes, including the Hōkūle'a. They didn't encounter doldrums or change their course to chase tattooed warriors. The Hōkūle'a made the trip from Nuku Hiva to Hawai'i in approximately 20 days.

Pueo is an *'aumakua* for many Hawai'ian families and is considered one of the most ancient of these guardians. There are tales of Pueo's bravery in battle and the owl's role in changing the outcome of historic events. In 1825 a naturalist sailed aboard a ship to, what Europeans called, the Sandwich Islands. In his studies, he recognized Pueo as a unique subspecies of short-eared owl found only on the Hawai'ian Islands. He gave the owl its Latin name, *Asio flammeus sandwichensis*. Pueo have a wing span of three to almost four feet and stand over a foot tall, but weigh only one pound. They are not the biggest bird on the islands, but you will never forget the first time you make eye contact with Pueo. Unlike most other owls they are active and hunt during the day. They also build their nests on the ground. This behavior puts them at great risk to predators like cats, dogs, and mongoose, animals that are not native to the Hawai'ian Islands. Their survival in modern times is also threatened by loss of habitat, exposure to pesticides, light pollution, and collisions with cars and trucks. Pueo's habitat merits conservation, which in turn will help protect other native species. The issues facing Hawai'i are not limited to the islands. It is important for all of us to reconnect, educate, and raise awareness for a more sustainable world. *Mālama honua.*

Glossary

Hawai'ian Word	Meaning
ahonui	To exercise patience, perseverance, or tolerate suffering.
'Alenuihāhā	Place name: The ocean channel between the islands of Hawai'i and Maui.
ama	Float of an outrigger canoe.
'aumakua	Family or personal god, deified ancestor who might assume the shape of a specific animal, insect, cloud, or plant. A special relationship exists between humans and their *'aumakua*; the *'aumakua* warns, guides, and even reprimands mortals through dreams, visions, and calls. (*'aumākua* pl.)
ali'i	Chief or ruler.
aloha	Love, compassion, empathy; a greeting; to love, to greet, hail or say hello. Greetings! Good-bye!
aumoe	Late at night. Literally time for bed.
'awa	An intoxicating drink made from the chewed root of the kava plant (*Piper spp.*)
Awaiāulu	To bind securely, fasten, like the bond of marriage. Title of a traditional love song.
'eā	Isn't that so? That's it!
'eia	Emphatic variation of *eia*. Here! Here it is!
hala	Plant introduced to Hawai'i by Polynesians. Hala tree, screwpine, *Pandanus tectorius*. Leaves grow at the stem tip and are used for weaving hats, mats, bags, but especially for weaving sails.
hale	House, building.
hānai	Foster child, adopted child, to raise, feed, or nourish.
Hawai'i	Refers to both the island and the state. The island is sometimes called the Big Island.

Hawai'ian Word	Meaning
Hawi	Place name: A rural town on the Kohala Coast, Hawai'i Island. Economy was mainly from the sugar planation established by missionaries in 1862. The Kohala Sugar Company operated until 1973.
he'e	Octopus.
heiau	Place of worship, shrine. Some are elaborate complexes of stone walls and platforms, others are small rock piles, standing stones, or earth terraces.
hele	To go, to move, to walk on.
Hilo	Place name: City on Hawai'i Island. Called Waiākea by the first Polynesian settlers, villages have been inhabited around the bay since AD 1100. Hilo became a major seaport for sugarcane commerce. A breakwater to protect the harbor was completed in 1929.
Hina	A goddess of many names and many forms, common to mythology in all the Pacific Islands. On the Marquesas, in one legend her brother compares her beauty to the moon.
Hoe aku i ka wa'a	Paddle ahead the canoe, also meaning; do your share, keep going.
ho'ōho	To exclaim, shout, haloo, or hūi.
ho'okolohe	To do – *ho'o* + *kolohe* – mischievous rascal or prankster. To play pranks; to do amusing things to create laughter.
Ho'ololi	To do – *ho'o* + *loli* – to change, alter, or transformation. Take a new form.
ho'omoe	To do – *ho'o* + *moe*, to sleep, to lie down.
Hōkūlani	Character name: *Hōkū* – star + *Lani* – heaven.
Honoka'a	Place name: A rural town on Hāmākua Coast, Hawai'i Island. Economy was mainly sugar production from 1873 to 1994.

Hawai'ian Word	Meaning
Honolulu	Place name: City on the south coast of the island of O'ahu. Polynesian settlers established villages and the area around the bay has been inhabited since AD 1100. It became the governmental seat to Hawai'ian kings and royalty beginning with Kamehameha I in 1804.
huki	Pull or tug.
'iako.	The boom of outrigger, also the number forty in counting.
Ikaika	Character name: Strong, powerful, sturdy.
Iolani Palace	Place name: Located in Honolulu. King Kamehameha III built Hale Ali'i, on this site in 1845. The Iolani (bird of Heaven) Palace was built by King Kalakaua in 1879-1882 for his wife, Queen Kapi'olani's 45th birthday. It was used as the capitol building until 1969.
kahuna	In reference to an expert in any field. Also means priest, sorcerer, magician.
Ka'imi	Character name: The one who searches or seeks.
Kā kākou	Ours, inclusive, (used for three or more.)
kanaka	Human being, man, person, individual.
kāne	Male.
Kapa'au	Place name: Rural town on the Kohala Coast, home to the original King Kamehameha I statue. Main economy was the Kohala Sugar Company 1862-1973.
kapa	*Tapa*, made from *wauke* (paper mullberry) or *māmaki* bark. Formerly clothing of any kind.
kapu	Taboo, prohibited, forbidden or restricted use.
kāua	Pronoun for we, us.
Kāulamana	Character name: *Kāula* – prophet, seer + *mana* – supernatural or divine power.
keiki	Child, little kid.

Hawai'ian Word	Meaning
Kekoa	Character name: *Ke* – the one + *koa* – to be brave or courageous.
Kele	Character name: To sail. A nickname, short for Ho'okele – a navigator.
Kiana	Character name: Hawai'ian given name for Diana.
ki'i akua	A small carved idol or image.
kīhei	Kapa garment, shawl, cape, like a sarong worn with the upper edge passed under one arm and knotted over the opposite shoulder.
Kō	Character name: Sugarcane, a plant introduced to Hawai'i by Polynesians. Secondary meaning is to pull, tug, or be wind-borne. A third meaning is to complete or come to fruition.
koa	Brave, fearless. Also an endemic forest tree *Acacia koa*, the largest and most valued of trees for canoes, surfboards, calabashes.
ko'i	An adze or ax-like tool.
kōlea	Pacific golden plover, a small migratory land bird (*Pluvialis dominica*). Migrates between Alaska and Hawai'i in 3-4 days non-stop flight.
kukui	Candlenut (*Aleurites moluccana*), Hawai'i state tree; also means lamp or light.
kuleana	Responsibility or right, privilege, interest or claim in. Often used in reference to lands and relations.
kupuna	Grandparent, grandmother or grandfather, relative, or close friend of your grandparent's generation, ancestor (singluar). *Kūpuna* is plural of kupuna.
laila	There. Following the particle, "*I*", directs attention, "at that place."
lānai	Porch, patio, veranda, balcony.

Hawai‘ian Word	Meaning
Lani	Character name: Heaven; in this story Lani is used as a nickname, short for *Hōkūlani*.
Lapa‘au	Character name: To heal, cure, practice or treat with medicine.
lau	Leaf.
lei	A garland or wreath of flowers, shells, feathers, seeds, or leaves, worn about the head or neck. eg. *Lei hulu*, a feather lei.
Līhau	Character name: Cool misty rain, moist and fresh like the dew.
Lili	Character name: Jealousy, envy, anger.
Li‘ulā	Character name: Twilight, mirage. This character is better known by his nickname, *Loloa*.
Loloa	Character name: The nickname for *Li‘ulā*, a boy who is short. The word comes from a reduplication of the word loa, when used in reference to a person, it means tall.
Lopaka	Character name: Hawai‘ian given name for Robert.
mahalo nui loa	Thank you very much.
Mahukona	Place name: A seaport on the Kohala Coast. A lighthouse was first erected in 1899, the harbor was important shipping point for sugar. A small town located there was abandoned in the 1950's and the harbor was closed in 1956. The site is now managed as Mahukona Beach Park.
maika‘i nō	Good, fine, alright, well, in good health.
Mākaukau	Character name: Able, handy, adept, skilled, preparation, to know how.
makuahine	Mother, aunt, female cousin, or relative in a parent's generation. (*Mākuahine* pl.)
mālama	To protect, preserve, save, caretaker, fidelity, or loyalty.

Hawai'ian Word	Meaning
Maloka	Character name: Skeptical, unbelieving.
Mamalahoa Highway	Place name: State Route 19, only sections of the original narrow and winding historic road remain along the Hāmākua Coast, some include narrow bridges over deep gulches.
mana	Spiritual, divine or supernatural power; to make or have such power, to give power to.
manō	Shark.
manu	Refers to bird, but referring to a canoe, it is the ornamental extensions at the stern and bow. To distinguish the back from front, the stern is manu hope, the forward bow is manu ihu.
mele	A song or chant of any kind, a poem.
Meli	Character name: Bee, honey.
Miki	Character name: To be quick, agile, or fast in work. Also can be used to indicate something that springs together, like the sides of a steel trap.
moena	A mat.
mo'o	In reference to canoes, the side planks fitted to the middle section on each side of a canoe hull.
mo'olelo	A story, a tale, a history or legend.
Mo'okini Heiau	Place name: This heiau is one of the oldest and most sacred heiaus in the Hawai'ian Islands, located on the North Kohala Coast, west of Hawi.
nai'a	Porpoise, dolphin.
niu	Plant introduced to Hawai'i by Polynesians. Coconut, the fruit of the coconut palm.
O'ahu	Place name: The most populated of all the Hawai'ian Islands. Scholars seem to agree that the name has no specific meaning. References to it as the Gathering Place in modern times are anecdotal.
'ohana	Family, relative, kin group, related.

Hawai'ian Word	Meaning
Pilipino	Filipino.
pola	In reference to canoes, the open deck between two hulls of a voyaging canoe.
pono	Correct, proper, moral, righteousness, fair, just, a moral quality.
pua'a	Pig, the animal. *Kalua pua'a*, pig baked in a pit oven.
Pueo	The Hawai'ian short-eared owl, endemic to the Hawai'ian Islands. *Asio flammeus sandwichensis.* They are revered and respected as *'aumakua* for many Hawai'ian families.
Pukikī	Portuguese.
pū'oleolē	Conch horn.
taro	Plant introduced to Hawai'i by Polynesians, called kalo. The root is used to make *poi*. In addition to a staple food source, also the center of spiritualism, mythology, and social structure in Hawai'ian culture.
ti	Plant introduced to Hawai'i by Polynesians, called kī. This plant traveled well in a canoe, as any section of a branch will root. Leaves used for cordage or clothing. Bundles used for thatching, or for plates at meals.
ūhini	Cricket, locust, or grasshopper.
'ukulele	Stringed instrument introduced to the islands by the Portuguese. Lit. translation is leaping flea.
'uala	Plant introduced to Hawai'i by Polynesians. The sweet potato is the only Polynesian-introduced plant that does not come from Southeast Asia, it comes from South America. There are many different theories on how this plant was introduced in ancient times to the Pacific islands.
uhu	Parrot fish. A reef dwelling fish. Some say that the colorful male is not as tasty as the reddish brown female.

Hawai'ian Word	Meaning
'ulu	Plant in the fig family introduced to Hawai'i by Polynesians. The breadfruit is an important food source on the Marquesas Islands because the trees can be grown on the steep mountain slopes. In Hawai'i the breadfruit is not as important as the taro.
wa'a	Canoe
wahine	Woman, singular. *Wāhine*, pl. women

There are many excellent internet resources to learn the multiple levels of meaning and the correct pronunciation of Hawai'ian words. The above information is provided only as an educational aid. You should listen to an authentic speaker and practice these words before using them in public!

For beginners, try using the following simple vowel sounds:

a sounds like ah, as in alone;
e sounds like eh, as in let;
i sounds like ee, as in bee;
o sounds like oh, as in okay;
u sounds like oo, as in school.

Diacritical marks, the kahakō and the 'okina, are important. The kahakō (or macron) is an emphatic elongation of the vowel sound, where ā becomes "Ahh". The 'okina is a consonant, not a punctuation mark. It is a glottal stop or breath break, similar to the pause between the two syllables in the English slang word "uh-oh".

Aloha

"Aloha Spirit" is the coordination of mind and heart
within each person. It brings each person to the self. Each
person must think and emote good feelings to others.
In the contemplation and presence of the life force,
"*Aloha*," the following *unuhi laula loa* may be used:

Akahai, meaning kindness, to be expressed with tenderness;
Lōkahi, meaning unity, to be expressed with harmony;
ʻOluʻolu, meaning agreeable, to be expressed with pleasantness;
Haʻahaʻa, meaning humility, to be expressed with modesty;
Ahonui, meaning patience, to be expressed with perseverance.

These are traits of character that express the charm,
warmth, and sincerity of Hawaiʻi's people.

Excerpt from H.R.S.§5-7.5, the Aloha Spirit Law.